A Flair for Beignets

A Flair for Beignets

A Sadie Kramer Flair Mystery

DEBORAH GARNER

CRANBERRY COVE PRESS

For all those who love mystery, beignets and café au lait—or any combination of the above.

BOOKS BY DEBORAH GARNER

The Paige MacKenzie Mystery Series

Above the Bridge
The Moonglow Café
Three Silver Doves
Hutchins Creek Cache
Crazy Fox Ranch

The Moonglow Christmas Novella Series

Mistletoe at Moonglow
Silver Bells at Moonglow
Gingerbread at Moonglow
Nutcracker Sweets at Moonglow
Snowfall at Moonglow

The Sadie Kramer Flair Series

A Flair for Chardonnay
A Flair for Drama
A Flair for Beignets
A Flair for Truffles
A Flair for Flip-Flops

Cranberry Bluff

ONE

Sadie fastened her seat belt, following the flight attendant's directions. She leaned back against the cushioned seat, pleased with the window location. Holding her tote bag securely in her lap, she looked out onto the runway as the plane taxied into takeoff position.

It would be good to get away, as much as she adored her life in San Francisco. She particularly loved running her fashion boutique, Flair, filled with unique apparel and accessories. The daily interaction with regular customers, as well as those discovering the shop for the first time, had kept her not only busy but entertained since becoming a widow years ago. Her assistant, Amber, was delightful to work with, not to mention the tantalizing plus of having her neighbor Matteo's chocolate shop, Ciocollato, right next door. What could be better than an existence filled with fashion and chocolate?

Actually, there were two additional aspects to her life that were even closer to her heart: the precious contents of her tote bag and a good adventure or mystery—not necessarily in a book either, though she appreciated a fictional detective who could follow a literary path of clues. Luckily, the treasure inside her tote often helped with her tendency to stumble upon mysteries herself. As if on cue, a tiny yip floated upward. Sadie hushed the source.

"Praline?"

Sadie turned toward the seat next to hers. She'd nodded to

the woman but said nothing when she first sat down, as an animated cell phone conversation was in progress. Now that the phone was turned off and stashed away, the woman held up a light brown, cookie-sized concoction that might as well have had the words "sugar rush" printed on it in bold letters. Granted, it wasn't chocolate, Sadie's most fervent addiction, but then again, it would be rude to turn it down, wouldn't it? *Yes, of course it would,* Sadie thought. She almost smacked her lips in anticipation of satisfying her sweet tooth. But she resisted as a matter of courtesy and accepted the offering gracefully.

"I don't mind if I do!" Sadie exclaimed, taking the sweet treat from the woman. "It looks delicious. Thank you. That's very kind of you to share." She took a nibble from the pale, bumpy, fudge-like cluster, closed her eyes, and sighed. "Oh my, pecans. I do love pecans."

"Clotile," the woman said.

Sadie opened her eyes. "Clotile? Is that a type of pecan?"

A smile crept across the woman's face, emphasizing wrinkles that gave away an age close to Sadie's own sixty-something years. "No, that's my name, Clotile. Clotile Laurent."

"Oh, of course!" Sadie said, taking another bite of the praline while noting the woman's stylish red hair and dangling necklace of multicolored beads. "Sadie here," she offered.

"Delighted to meet you," Clotile said. She pulled another praline out of a small bag and took a bite. "I never travel without a supply of Lisette's pralines. Makes me feel I'm not far from home even if I am."

"And where is home?" Sadie asked.

"New Orleans," Clotile said. "And you?"

"San Francisco," Sadie answered. "I'm on my way to New Orleans." As soon as the destination tumbled out of her mouth, she felt foolish. It was obvious where the plane was headed. "Is Lisette a friend of yours? Or a sister, perhaps?"

"Oh, no." Clotile laughed. "Well, I suppose you could call her a friend, at least an acquaintance. She owns Chez Lisette Patisserie. I go there every morning for my café au lait." I'm a regular customer."

"Well, I can certainly see why, if everything she serves is this delicious," Sadie said, finishing off the praline. She licked her lips to gather up any lingering trace of sugar. "I may have just become a regular myself, and I don't even know where her place is."

Clotile laughed. "It's in the French Quarter, not hard to find. You must go there."

"I'm staying in that area," Sadie said. "I'll have to make a point of visiting her bakery." Sadie paused. "It's a bakery, right?"

Clotile nodded. "Yes, actually a bakery and a café. They serve a delicious lunch too. But the pastries and sweets are the main draw."

Sadie stole a peek sideways. Seated alongside Clotile, she could only take in a partial view, but the woman was slender enough to not look like she spent much time at a bakery, indulging in sweets. Maybe Clotile was one of those people with high metabolisms that she'd always envied. Sadie, however, was quite certain she could gain a pound just by smelling the enticing aromas wafting from a bakery doorway as she passed by. Not that she often passed by, that is. Sweets were like magnets to her.

"Will you be staying long?" Clotile asked.

"A week: six nights, seven days," Sadie said. "Long enough to see the sights, take in local flavor, and relax."

"We should exchange phone numbers—if you'd like, of

course," Clotile said. "We could meet up at Chez Lisette Patisserie for coffee—and something sweet to go with it, naturally."

"Absolutely," Sadie said. She pulled her cell phone out of her tote bag, which resulted in a tiny yip. A passing flight attendant sent a questioning look in Sadie's direction. Sadie waved her cell phone in the air. "Silly ringtone!" she exclaimed. The flight attendant directed Sadie to turn her cell phone off, then walked away, a dubious expression on her face.

"We'll exchange numbers later," Clotile said. She lowered her voice, leaned toward Sadie with a conspiratorial grin, and whispered, "What's his name?"

Sadie sat up, noting the flight attendant had moved down the aisle. "Her," she whispered as she leaned toward Clotile. "Coco." She thought about letting Clotile peek inside her tote bag but knew it would result in another yip. "I'll introduce you later."

"Where are you staying?" Clotile asked and then immediately backpedaled. "Oh, I'm sorry, you just met me, and you're traveling, and… I should know better than to ask that." She shook her head, and Sadie could tell Clotile was sincere. A sense of friendship had been evident from the beginning of the conversation.

"No, that's fine," Sadie said. "I reserved a room at Hotel Arnaud-LeBlanc. A suite, actually—I decided to splurge on this trip, make it a true vacation."

"Ah, Hotel Arnaud-LeBlanc," Clotile said, an odd expression on her face.

Sadie frowned, confused by Clotile's reaction. "Why? Is it not a good place? The reviews are excellent, and it sounded like it had an interesting history. I do love historic hotels."

"Oh, no, it's fabulous," Clotile said. "I've attended events in their courtyard, which is used for wedding receptions, garden parties... that sort of thing."

"Then why the odd look when I said the name?" Sadie asked. "I could change to another hotel, if you think I should."

"No, no reason to do that," Clotile said. "It's just funny that's where you're staying." She sighed and let her head rest against the back of her seat, smiling.

"Why is that?" Sadie asked. Clotile's relaxed demeanor was reassuring, but her initial reaction had piqued Sadie's curiosity.

"It's just an odd coincidence," Clotile said. She patted Sadie's armrest with one hand, an elegant ruby ring catching the overhead lighting. "LeBlanc is the family name of Bluette LeBlanc. The hotel's been in their family for three generations."

"Okay," Sadie said, not following at all.

"Bluette LeBlanc—as in Bluette's Beignets—is Lisette's biggest competitor," Clotile explained. "There's tension between the two bakeries, going back generations."

"Like a Hatfield-McCoy scenario?" Sadie pondered the old rivalry between the Kentucky and West Virginia families. "Is Arnaud..." Sadie paused, thinking this through. "Is that Lisette's family name? Do the bakery families own the hotel?" More and more, it sounded like changing hotels might not be a bad idea.

"No, no," Clotile said, shaking her head. "Nothing like that. Mimi Arnaud is a regular customer at Lisette's place, but Lisette isn't related to either family."

"Hmm," Sadie said. "I'd think she'd want to frequent both bakeries, if they're as fabulous as you say. Then again, maybe she does go to both, though she might prefer the food at Lisette's, or..." At this point, Sadie was talking to herself and was almost startled when Clotile spoke up.

"Mimi won't have anything to do with Bluette's place,"

Clotile said. "It's a shame, really, since both bakeries serve delicious food."

The flight attendant passed by again, handing out small packages of cookies. Sadie waited until she moved on before opening it and dropping one into her tote bag. She coughed to cover up the yip of thanks that she knew would follow.

"It sounds like I might have to visit both," Sadie said. "You know, just to do some taste-testing in order to better understand the rivalry."

"Of course," Clotile said. "You won't hear me disagree with that."

Sadie watched as Clotile pulled a book out of her carry-on bag.

"*Murder on the Orient Express*," Sadie said, reading the book cover. "A classic."

"Yes." Clotile nodded her head. "I can't resist a good murder mystery."

"I understand completely," Sadie said. "Those seem to fall right into my lap." Thinking back to recent trips to Napa Valley and Monterey Bay, she thought it best not to mention that they sometimes weren't limited to printed pages.

Sadie smiled and looked out the window, leaving Clotile to enjoy reading. Thick puffs of white clouds below suddenly reminded her of cotton candy. Yes, she would make sure to visit both bakeries. Any excuse to follow a trail of sweets was a good one, as far as she was concerned. The possibility of long-standing family intrigue was just an added bonus.

TWO

Tipping the bellman for delivering her luggage, Sadie closed the door to her two-room suite and looked around with approval. The pastel-colored finishes of the antique French provincial furnishings lent a peaceful ambiance to the elegant space. A mahogany settee with traditionally curved cabriole legs rested against one wall, its upholstery a dusty pink hue reminiscent of roses she'd passed in the courtyard on her way from the lobby. Two Louis XV armchairs graced the area in front of a small fireplace. A pine French country hutch with wrought iron detail displayed dishes and knickknacks inside glass doors.

Sadie set her tote bag on the woven rush seat of a ladder-backed chair, one of two that flanked a simple mahogany table with a slight scalloped design along the edge. Coco's tiny head popped out immediately. After giving Sadie a look of reprimand—after all, she'd been in the tote bag much longer than she would have preferred—she jumped down and explored the new digs. Finding a low ottoman in a rose tone that matched the settee, she hopped up and curled in a contented ball, a satisfied look on her furry Yorkie face.

"I don't think so, Coco," Sadie said. "These are expensive pieces of furniture, and I did ship your pet palace out here in advance." Although Coco raised her eyebrows in question, Sadie felt no guilt. Coco's usual travel kennel—which kept her out of trouble in hotel rooms—was about as high-class as possible. Outfitted with velvet cushions and china food and water dishes, the petite canine could hardly complain. "We'll set it up in the other room, near the bed. Speaking of which, let's go check that room out."

Coco followed patiently as Sadie walked down a short hallway about five feet in length. A full bath sat off to the right side while a narrow table with intricate grape leaf carvings flanked the left. Coco veered off into the bathroom and hopped into a claw-foot tub. Wagging her tail in approval, she jumped back out and followed Sadie to the bedroom. Her ears perked up as Sadie gasped.

"Coco, this is magnificent!" Sadie said, delighted. "Your travel palace can go right beside this sleigh bed—a wonderful style, I must say. It's low enough that you can jump up and sit next to me while I read at night." She made a mental note to ask the hotel clerk for an old sheet to cover the bedspread. As much as she hated the idea of covering up the design, she'd dislike any damage that Coco might do even more.

A knock at the door signaled the arrival of Coco's own accommodation. Again Sadie tipped the bellman and brought the lavish kennel into the bedroom. After unfolding and setting it up, she filled one Villeroy and Boch bowl with water and tossed a treat in the other, as it was too early for dinner. Coco trotted inside the open door, debated the treat as a form of bribery, ate it anyway, and took her place dramatically on a velvet cushion, as if it were a compromise over Sadie's bedspread.

"Just deal with it, Coco," Sadie said, feeling humorous as she kicked off her shoes and stretched out on the sleigh bed. Looking around, she admired the printed linen toile window treatments, which featured peaceful pastoral scenes. The overall effect of the suite's décor was relaxing, exactly as she'd hoped. As if it couldn't get any better, a glance at her nightstand revealed a small box, tied with gold ribbon, compliments of the hotel. Opening it, she found six petite truffles, each a different culinary masterpiece. She popped one in her mouth and closed her eyes, savoring its delicious lemon crème flavor. This rivaled Matteo's own chocolates back home, not that she would dare tell him that.

Tempting as it was to take another bite of chocolate, a rare moment of willpower struck her. She had five more nights in New Orleans, and there were five more truffles. She'd save one for each night. Besides, she hadn't had dinner yet. There was no point in spoiling her appetite in a city brimming with delicious dining options. She retied the gold ribbon as a reminder of her resolve and set the box aside.

"Speaking of dining," Sadie said aloud, as if she'd been conversing with Coco about this very topic already. She paused as Coco tilted her head to one side, begging inclusion in Sadie's thought process. "We haven't eaten a normal meal since we left San Francisco. Those cookies in transit just didn't do the trick." Coco smacked her lips approvingly at the mention of cookies. "Let's dress up and go out, explore the town," Sadie said. She hopped up, opened her suitcase, and began rummaging through articles of clothing. Choosing a bright red tunic, rhinestone-studded jeans, and a denim vest with interior pockets, she quickly changed. She switched Coco's usual hot pink collar for a red one to match her own outfit. Scooping the dog up, she settled Coco inside her tote bag and zipped her money inside her vest. Prepared for the raucous reputation of Bourbon Street, the two headed out— Sadie on foot, Coco and the tote bag firmly held against Sadie's stomach.

Six blocks later, Sadie paused in front of a café sign on

Bourbon Street. "Red beans and rice," she said to Coco. The Yorkie poked her head out of the tote bag and looked around. Apparently, this did not meet with approval, as Coco tucked her head back inside.

"Fine," Sadie said. She continued along the pedestrian street, then paused front of another eatery. "Red beans and rice," she read from the menu posted outside. Coco didn't even bother to stick her head out.

Three doors later, Sadie paused again. "Okay, Coco, I'm telling you right now you're going to have to go along with this one, whether you like it or not." She recited multiple menu items from a chalkboard posted on the wall outside. "Jambalaya, shrimp po-boy, seafood gumbo, chargrilled oysters..." Sadie scanned additional choices, already edging toward the door. Once inside, she was greeted by a young hostess and escorted to a comfortable booth alongside a far wall. Within minutes, a glass of water landed on the table and a well-dressed waiter in his early twenties stood before her. His name tag was shaped like a crawfish and read Charles.

"Would you care for a drink to start and perhaps some of our Cajun turtle soup?"

The dual question gave Sadie pause. A drink sounded good, but she felt iffy about the soup. Not wanting to show ignorance by asking if there really was turtle in the soup, she ordered a gin and tonic and asked for more time to look over the menu. Halfway through the tantalizing descriptions, her cell phone buzzed with an incoming text.

All settled in? Meet for coffee at Chez Lisette Patisserie tomorrow?

Sadie wasn't at all surprised to hear from Clotile already. When they'd parted ways at the airport earlier, both felt as if they'd known each other for years.

Sure. What time? Out at dinner now. Sadie clicked Send.

Great, your first dinner out here. Have red beans and rice with whatever you order.

Sadie grinned. *Will do. Thinking seafood gumbo. Do you recommend?* Again, she hit Send, noticing the waiter approaching the table with a pad of paper and pen.

Excellent choice. Enjoy. Nine a.m. for coffee at Chez Lisette Patisserie?

"I'll have the seafood gumbo," Sadie said to Charles. She covered the cell's microphone with one hand as she spoke but quickly realized the gesture was absurd. "With a side order of red beans and rice." She turned back to her cell phone and sent another text. *Sounds good.*

Need directions?

Sadie shook her head, yet another ridiculous response. Would she ever get used to these newfangled phones? *No thanks. Will Google it. See you then.* There, she told herself. She was a modern woman, after all.

Ten minutes later, Sadie took her first taste of the gumbo, then a second, then a third. Delighted, she waved her napkin at Charles, calling the waiter over to the table.

"My, this is exceptional!" Sadie exclaimed. "What exactly is in it?"

Charles laughed. "You might as well just ask what *isn't* in it," he said. "It might be a shorter list."

"Yes, I can see that," Sadie said, eyeing the large bowl in front of her. She poked at it with a fork in one hand and a spoon in the other, picking out random pieces for analysis. "Obviously there's shrimp and crab and some kind of whitefish."

"Red snapper today," the waiter said, "although sometimes we use cod or pollack."

"Obviously tomatoes and... bell peppers, I think—

something green," Sadie continued.

"Yes," Charles said. "Green peppers, also scallions and okra."

Sadie looked up. "And about fifty spices!"

"Indeed," the waiter said. "Well, maybe not quite that many, but yes: spices galore."

"Well, I approve wholeheartedly," Sadie said. After Charles walked away, she dug in, alternating the gumbo with the red beans and rice and enjoying every bite. Contrary to her usual dining habits, she turned down dessert, certain her visit to the bakery in the morning would make up for whatever she would have ordered after the meal.

A leisurely walk back to the hotel gave her time to take in the ambiance on Bourbon Street. Jazz music floated out from bars and eateries, and neon signs lit up windows filled with NOLA souvenirs. Tourists strolled along, frozen daiquiris in hand. Iconic locations caught her attention, such as Pat O'Brien's bar, and Marie Laveau's House of Voodoo.

"Look, Coco," Sadie said, reading a sign in a window next to Marie Laveau's. "Maybe we should have our fortunes read. What do you think?" She listened to Coco's yipped response. "Well, I don't know about that," Sadie said. She looked down at the top of the tote bag as she spoke, earning strange looks from a man and woman passing by. "You have a good point there, Coco," she continued after the couple walked away. "I'm not sure if they can read the fortunes of dogs, but it's worth a try. Who knows what the lines in your paw might foretell?"

Patting her tote bag as one might pat a baby to keep it calm, Sadie entered the shop and approached a sales counter. The girl behind the counter looked barely out of her teens, perhaps a college student working part-time to help pay tuition.

"We'd like to have our fortunes told."

The young girl looked to Sadie's left and then to her right, undoubtedly trying to identify the "we" in Sadie's statement. Not curious enough to ask, she simply glanced toward the back of the store, indicating a beaded curtain. "We have a new fortune-teller. Gina is new in town but in tune with the spirit world. She will tell you all you need to know."

Sadie thanked the girl and headed for the back, passing rows of voodoo dolls, miniature alligator heads, and a variety of other items that struck her as bizarre.

The beads rustled as Sadie stepped through, and she had to pause to detach a few strands that became tangled with her tote bag. Once inside, she looked around, taking in the dimly lit room. The space was small, just large enough for two velvet armchairs to sit on each side of a glass table. Strings of twigs, small leather pouches, and faded feather boas hung from the walls at contrasting levels. Images from movie scenes and books flitted through her mind, and she briefly expected to see a crystal ball in the center of the table. Instead, the surface was clear, aside from a deck of tarot cards.

A small side door opened, and a woman stepped in, dressed in a flowing skirt and tunic, with a fringed shawl around her neck. Her hair was long and thick and hung loosely around her shoulders like a mop. A few strands intertwined with multiple gold chains that rested against her tunic. Several crystals hung from the longest chain. A cluster of bangles adorned one wrist, as well as a bracelet of skull beads that glowed softly. She made a note to find one like that in a souvenir shop. It would amuse people she knew back in San Francisco.

"I am Gina," the woman said softly as she approached a chair. One hand encircled the crystals that dangled in front of her shawl. The other indicated the other chair, bangles and skull beads clinking against each other as she invited Sadie to take a seat. "You are here to have your fortune told," she said, a statement Sadie was certain she'd repeated hundreds of times, if not thousands.

"Yes, we are," Sadie said, taking a seat in what turned out to be a surprisingly comfortable chair. She eased back against plush padded velvet, placing her tote bag on her lap and settling in. Between the dim lighting, the fortune-teller's soft voice, and the cushy chair, she wondered briefly if she might fall asleep.

The woman repeated the sales girl's exact movements, looking first to Sadie's right, and then to her left. "You are not alone," she said, redirecting her gaze to Sadie.

My, this woman is good, Sadie thought. She fought back an urge to grin and to counter with a sassy reply. However, no response was necessary, as Coco's ears, eyes, and nose suddenly popped up above the rim of the tote bag. Coco tilted her furry head to the side and eyed the unfamiliar woman with curiosity. Both Coco and the fortune-teller blinked.

"I see," Gina said, a slight smile emerging on the otherwise serious face. "Well, I think we can manage that." She gathered the tarot cards, shuffled them, and then laid them out one by one, each bringing a pause and declaration. "You are on a journey."

Yes, I think that's obvious.

"You are only passing through briefly."

Well, it is a vacation, after all.

"The winds of change are approaching." Each statement was delivered calmly and routinely until one card caused the fortune-teller to pause and frown.

"I sense sadness."

Way off base, but I'll play along, Sadie thought.

"Well, I do miss my neighbor's chocolate store." It was something to say, after all.

Gina stifled a look of annoyance but continued.

"I can feel something else. You are unhappy in your travels. Perhaps something you ate? Or you've landed roughly…" Gina paused, eyes closed. "Your means of transportation… no, your accommodations… or perhaps…"

Sadie held back a sigh. This was fun but getting to be enough. "I'm sure you're right," she said, not wanting to be rude, "but it must be something else. My flight was fine, the seafood gumbo was delicious, and the Hotel Arnaud-LeBlanc is charming."

The fortune-teller's expression then became more serious. It struck Sadie that the woman's acting ability was better than she'd given her credit for. Instead of being annoyed with Sadie contradicting her previous statement, she looked genuinely afraid.

"This is not good." Gina shuffled in her seat. "I'm sorry. I don't like it when the cards foretell danger, but I cannot ignore what they tell me."

"What is it?" Sadie asked, not sure whether to be entertained or worried.

Gina shook her head, as if trying to shake away a feeling, but her expression remained the same. "I'm afraid someone is in grave danger." She paused, frowning. "Someone you know, or… that you will know." Again, she shook her head. "I'm sorry. I'm not sure."

"Will my palm tell you more?" Sadie extended her arm. Gina took it cautiously and traced the lines, which caused a tickling sensation that briefly lightened the somber mood.

"It appears you will have a long life," Gina said, looking relieved.

"And what about Coco," Sadie said. She gently lifted Coco out of the tote bag and set her on the table. Coco hesitantly allowed Gina to examine her paw.

"Also a long life," Gina said. She smiled and took a look at Coco's other paw. "And many treats," she added, much to Coco's delight. The Yorkie bestowed a slurp of appreciation on the fortune-teller's hand. Gina thanked Coco and then turned to Sadie. "I don't know anything more."

"Thank you," Sadie said. She stood, settled Coco back in the tote, and started toward the exit, turning back once more. "This was fun." Sadie tried not to notice the worried look on the fortune-teller's face.

Yes, Sadie thought as she left the fortune-teller's shop, *this was simply a bit of fun. Right?*

THREE

Chez Lisette Patisserie was as charming as Sadie expected it to be, its appeal accentuated by the sweet aroma of sugary baked goods. Stepping into the café felt like entering another world. As opposed to the modern tables, counter seats, and occasional armchairs of big-city coffee haunts, Chez Lisette offered old-fashioned café tables and chairs. The side walls boasted floor-to-ceiling murals of outdoor scenes, such that customers might feel like they were seated on the outside patio of a Parisian café along the Champs-Élysée. Sadie half expected to look to her side and see the Arc de Triomphe out the window.

The line at the register was long but dwindled while Sadie eagerly scanned the contents of the display cases. She couldn't recall ever seeing such an extravagant, tempting assortment of croissants. Notecards in front of each tantalizing tray announced enticing flavors in scrolled calligraphy: almond, raspberry-peach, boysenberry and, of course, chocolate. Each perfectly formed croissant was stacked artfully on a mountain of similar items. White paper doilies with scalloped edges decorated the base of each mouthwatering stack of baked delicacies. The glass shelf just below held trays of puffed, ball-shaped pastries dusted with powdered sugar. A sign with calligraphy that matched the croissant notecards presented these tantalizing creations as "BTBs." Small lettering below spelled out Blissfully Tasty Beignets.

"Don't fall for that BTB description," a voice behind Sadie whispered after she took a place in line. She turned to see Clotile had joined her. "Everyone knows it really stands for Better than Bluette's."

"Seriously?" Sadie's eyebrows lifted. "The rivalry is that intense?"

Clotile nodded and leaned closer, lowering her voice even more. "Oh yes, absolutely. You should see the shelf tortes called 'BTLs' at Bluette's place."

"Dare I ask?" Sadie said.

"Best Tasting Linzer, supposedly," Clotile said. "But you know it means Better than Lisette's."

The line moved forward as Sadie contemplated this information. "Are the bakeries situated close to each other?"

Clotile laughed. "You could say that." She nodded toward the front window. Sadie followed her gesture, noticing for the first time that another bakery sat just across the street.

"Oh dear," Sadie said. "That must be awkward."

"Awkward but convenient for battle," Clotile said. "If Lisette puts a sign in the window, Bluette responds with one that is a tiny bit bigger. If Bluette opens her front door to let the bakery aromas float out to the sidewalk, Lisette opens not only her door but her windows too."

A petite woman at the register greeted Sadie. She wore basic jeans and a T-shirt, both partially covered by an apron that said Kiss the cook.

"Good morning, Lisette," Clotile said, peeking around Sadie. "This is a new friend of mine. Ring everything together; I'll pay."

"How kind," Sadie said, "but not necessary. I'm happy to pay."

"Nonsense," Clotile said.

Lisette laughed and smiled at Sadie. "There's no point in arguing with Clotile, my dear."

Sadie gave in, ordered a chocolate croissant and café mocha, and thanked Clotile.

"And I'll take a cinnamon BTB and café au lait," Clotile said. She pulled a twenty out of a shoulder bag and handed it to Lisette, who gave back change along with the baked goods. "I'll bring your drinks out when they're ready," she said.

Sadie and Clotile moved away from the counter, pastries in hand, and settled at a small table along one side of the café. A colorful mural on the wall showed a railing and street scene, giving the table a semblance of a balcony location.

A jangle of bells from the direction of the café entrance caused Sadie to glance at the front door as a woman entered. Sadie took in her slightly graying hair and guessed her to be in her midforties. Wearing a plain dress and cardigan sweater in subdued colors, the woman took a seat on the opposite side of the café.

"Interesting," Sadie remarked to Clotile as she tilted her head toward the other table. "The woman who just entered didn't order anything at the counter. She simply sat down."

Clotile looked across the café, following Sadie's gesture. "Oh, that's Mimi Arnaud. She's quiet, keeps to herself. She always has the same thing—actually, two of the same thing, some kind of tart. She'll eat one and then work on crossword puzzles and then eat the other. Quite the creature of habit, but that's how some customers are. She doesn't need to order; Lisette knows what to bring out to her."

"You said her name is Mimi... Arnaud? As in...?" Sadie left the question unfinished as Clotile had already begun to nod her head.

"Yes," Clotile said. "As in Hotel Arnaud-LeBlanc, where

you're staying. You'll probably see her around the hotel. She still does the books and does the hiring and firing. I guess she pretty much runs the place."

"And LeBlanc is…"

"Yes," Clotile repeated. "As in Bluette LeBlanc."

"I see," Sadie said as she took a bite of her croissant. She closed her eyes in delight at the taste of the smooth chocolate filling and then continued. "Mimi Arnaud always eats here, you say. She never eats across the street at Bluette's place?"

"Absolutely not," Clotile said. "She won't step foot inside there."

"Because of the old hotel rivalry?" Sadie raised an eyebrow.

The conversation paused as Lisette approached the table with a tray and set the café au lait and café mocha down. Sadie noticed a small pot of tea with lemon, along with two raspberry tarts, remained on the tray.

"My, those look delicious," Sadie said, eyeing the baked goods.

"The raspberry-almond tarts? We still have some left in the display case," Lisette said. "If you'd like one of these, I'll just grab another for the customer."

"I'd better not," Sadie said, patting her ample belly. "But I dare say they look tempting. She thanked Lisette for the offer and was not surprised to see the café owner head to Mimi's table next to deliver the tarts and accompanying tea. The two women exchanged a few quiet words that Sadie couldn't overhear, and then Lisette returned to the counter to serve a customer waiting in line.

"To answer your question from a minute ago, no, Mimi will not have breakfast anywhere but here," Clotile said. "I suspect part of the reason she comes here every day is just to annoy Bluette. Although she must love those tarts. That's the only thing she ever orders, always with a pot of tea."

"I saw those in the display case when I first came in," Sadie said. "If I didn't have such an addiction to chocolate, I might have ordered one myself."

"You could always take one to go," Clotile suggested. "Perhaps for a midnight snack later tonight in your hotel room."

"Not a bad idea," Sadie said. It had already occurred to her that a couple of to-go items might come in handy later. She could always grab coffee or tea from the hotel lobby to accompany the treats. "Tell me more about the Arnaud-LeBlanc feud." She took a sip of her café mocha and waited for more information from Clotile.

"I don't know much, and what I know is mostly based on word of mouth," Clotile said. "The families have never been very forthcoming with specifics, and newspaper articles have always seemed like speculation to me, without any details."

"Isn't that sort of odd?" Sadie said.

Clotile shrugged. "I don't know. Some families are more tight-lipped about their secrets. All I know is there was some kind of falling-out between Mimi's grandfather and Bluette's father. The Arnauds and LeBlancs have been at a standoff ever since."

"Over money, perhaps…," Sadie mused.

"I wouldn't be surprised," Clotile said. "Most disputes seem to boil down to disagreements over money, one way or another, especially in business."

Sadie nodded. "I suppose so." More than one such crisis amidst clients of her late husband's real estate business crossed her mind.

A light cough interrupted Sadie's thoughts and drew her attention to Mimi Arnaud's table. The woman had finished off the first tart and pushed the plate to the side. A newspaper was open, spread across the table. She took a sip of water and then picked up a pencil, touched the tip to the newsprint, and began to write.

"Daily crossword puzzle," Clotile said. "She always does it. I don't have the patience for it, myself. There are always a few words I can't figure out, which just frustrates me."

Sadie nodded, never having been fond of crossword puzzles herself.

Clotile and Sadie returned to discussing the possible causes of the Arnaud-LeBlanc rivalry. Sadie offered suggestions of conflicts that had a way of destroying business partnerships. Clotile ventured opinions on each potential scenario.

Again, Mimi coughed. This time she stood up and headed over to a side table where water was available for all customers. She refilled her glass, took a sip, and carried it back to her table, pausing at one point to rest her hand on the back of a chair, as if to catch her balance.

"My," Clotile said. "I wonder if Mimi has taken to drinking in the morning. She seems a bit unsteady on her feet."

"I noticed that too," Sadie said. "But then my balance isn't what it used to be in my younger days."

"Good point," Clotile said. "Neither is mine. That makes me wonder about all those hills in San Francisco. Aren't those difficult to walk up and down, at least compared to years ago?"

"A little," Sadie admitted. "I'm enjoying the flat walking areas here in New Orleans."

The discussion continued as Clotile and Sadie bantered comparisons of their respective cities back and forth—hills versus flatland, sourdough bread versus beignets, and the Golden Gate Bridge versus long, flat stretches of roadway over water.

"Oh, and the crab cocktails along Fisherman's Wharf…" Sadie paused, noticing Mimi waving one arm above her head, motioning toward the front counter. Lisette responded by holding her index finger up in the air, a signal to wait while she finished giving change to a well-dressed gentleman in line. When the man headed for the front door, Lisette hurried over to Mimi's table.

"What do you think is the matter?" Sadie asked, worried for the older woman.

"I don't know," Clotile said, equally concerned.

Sadie could see Mimi attempting to explain something while grasping the edge of the table with two hands. Lisette leaned forward, as if not able to understand what the woman was saying. Abruptly Mimi's eyes widened, as if hit by a sudden realization. She opened her mouth to explain but instead fell forward, planting her forehead firmly in the half-eaten tart, a splatter of raspberries and whipped cream alongside her immobile head. A collective gasp circled the room. Several people jumped up but didn't move, each at a loss as to how to help. One customer pounded lightly on Mimi's back and then attempted several ill-trained Heimlich maneuvers, which simply pulled Mimi's face up out of, and back into, the pastry repeatedly.

"I'm a doctor," the gentleman at the door said, turning back and rushing to Mimi's table. He lifted the woman from the chair, laid her in the aisle, and pressed his fingers to her neck, trying to find a pulse. Finally he looked up at a panic-stricken Lisette and shook his head. "I'm sorry. She's gone."

Around the room, customers sat back, stunned, and exchanged looks with each other. Clotile and Sadie bore the same shocked expression on their faces as the others.

Shifting in her chair, Sadie picked up her tote bag and

clutched it in her lap, as if to protect Coco from the traumatic event. She pushed her half-empty café au lait toward the center of the table and turned to Clotile.

"I think I'll skip those tarts to go after all."

FOUR

Sadie paced back and forth in her hotel room as Coco looked on. The Yorkie's head swiveled, watching Sadie's movements sympathetically, in spite of not knowing what had provoked them.

"I don't understand it, Coco," Sadie said. "The woman was fine when she walked in and dead within the hour." She paused, as if waiting for Coco to respond, and then resumed pacing. "Oh, and to think I almost ordered one of those tarts to go!" She shuddered. "Then again," she continued, "maybe the poor woman's demise had nothing to do with the tart itself. Maybe she simply choked."

Clotile and Sadie had lingered at the patisserie until the EMTs and police arrived, mostly to attempt to console Lisette, who was hysterical. The bakery owner sat huddled at the table with Clotile and Sadie as an officer asked her questions and jotted down notes. Lisette answered as best she could. No, she hadn't sensed anything wrong with Mimi when she first arrived. No, there was no one new working in the kitchen. Yes, other customers had ordered the same tarts that morning and had not suffered any ill effects. No, only a few people had keys to the bakery, and she trusted every single one completely.

After the police had finished questioning everyone present and the coroner had taken Mimi's body away, Lisette broke down, her hysterics turning to sobs. "How could this happen?" she cried. "She seemed fine when she arrived."

"What did she say when she waved you over?" Clotile asked.

"She said something was wrong, that she felt dizzy and hot," Lisette said. "But her speech was slurred. It was hard to understand her."

"It wasn't your fault," Clotile said, attempting to console her.

"Oh my!" Lisette cried, one hand flying up to cover her mouth. "I didn't even think of that. Maybe that's what the police will think. After all, I'm the one who served her the food. Oh my!" she repeated. "Maybe that's what *everyone* will think: my customers, my friends!"

"Try not to jump to conclusions," Sadie said. "This has been enough of a shock as it is."

"Yes," Clotile added, patting her friend's arm to reassure her. "You know there will be a full investigation. They'll get to the bottom of this, and you'll be cleared."

"And meanwhile?" Lisette's sobbing ebbed, and her voice softened. "I can't open the bakery. The detective said they'd need to go through the whole kitchen, every ingredient, every utensil. And will my customers even come back when I reopen?"

Sadie had to agree it was a good question. This was certainly not a situation where the saying "there's no such thing as bad publicity" applied. A customer had dropped dead—literally—in the middle of a raspberry-almond tart. It hardly constituted positive advertising for the patisserie.

Now, while pacing the floor of her hotel suite, Sadie tried to piece together what little information she knew.

"Who would have wanted to harm Mimi Arnaud, Coco? Clotile seemed to think she was a nice woman, quiet but not disliked. At least she didn't say so." Sadie paused, as if expecting an opinion from the petite canine. Coco simply licked one paw and then yawned. "Then again, maybe she had enemies that Clotile didn't know about."

The buzz of an incoming text interrupted Sadie's thoughts. Knowing it would either be Amber, from her San Francisco boutique, or Clotile, she picked up the phone. It was Clotile.

Interesting development.

Sadie responded, curious.

What happened?

She watched the little dots on the screen as Clotile typed an answer, feeling the sense of impatience that always accompanied the anticipation of an incoming text.

I stayed with Lisette to help her close up.

Sadie nodded at the phone, which she immediately realized was silly, as Clotile could not see her gesture.

And? How is she?

Sadie sighed after sending the text. It was a ridiculous question. Clearly, Lisette couldn't be okay after the events of the morning.

She's upset, went home to rest. But that's not what I wanted to tell you.

Again, Sadie paused, waiting for more.

I looked across the street while waiting for Lisette and saw a face peeking out from behind a curtain.

"Huh," Sadie said aloud. What point could Clotile be trying to make? There was nothing odd about that. Of course others would notice the activity and look out.

Seems normal, under the circumstances, Sadie typed.

Not this, Clotile responded. *It was only a face; the rest of the person was hidden behind the curtain. I'm sure it was Bluette. Short gray hair, glasses.*

Normal, Sadie thought to herself. Neighbors would be curious to see an ambulance and police car coming and going on their block. But then again…

Are you saying what I think you are? That the other bakery owner is involved?

Clotile replied, *Could be. The Arnaud-LeBlanc dispute, you know.*

That fierce of a grudge? Sadie typed.

Clotile's answer was short. *Yes.*

Sadie set the phone down to think for a minute, a luxury afforded by text that wouldn't have been otherwise. She opened Coco's travel palace and gave her a treat, then returned to the phone. *Want to come by the hotel later? Wine-and-appetizer hour 5-7.*

Sounds good, Clotile answered. *Day plans?* She added, *I can offer suggestions.*

Sadie smiled. It was a nice offer but not needed. *French Market,* she typed back.

Perfect, Clotile replied. *Enjoy. See you later.*

* * *

The French Market, a short walk from the hotel, was abuzz with activity when Sadie arrived. She'd read about the famed marketplace before but wasn't prepared for the delightfully unique atmosphere. Vendors and goods stretched for blocks, tables brimming with everything from handmade voodoo dolls to alligator heads. Tall racks displayed masks so varied that Sadie had the odd impression that each held a personality within. Shelves and counters offered spicy varieties of hot sauces and herbal mixtures. The unusual variety of offerings had Sadie immediately weighing carry-on luggage options for her trip home. Surely a fanciful mask with ribbon streamers would look good on the wall in her San Francisco penthouse.

Not all the tables and booths were filled with oddities. A farmer's market section offered fresh fruits and vegetables, artisan bread, homemade jellies, and pralines. Local artists displayed pottery, paintings, and jewelry. The wide variety of merchandise, mixed with excited crowds of people and festive music, filled Sadie with energy.

"Coco, what do you think about one of these?" Sadie directed her question toward her tote bag as she fingered one of many colorful feather boas hanging from a grid. "Hot pink or blue? Or maybe orange?" Coco's head popped up above the rim of the tote. She sniffed the row of fluffy objects and then batted one with a paw. "All right," Sadie said. "Blue it is then." She fished a wallet out of the bag and paid the vendor. Placing the boa around her neck, she flipped one end over her shoulder and flounced her way onward.

The crowd seemed to multiply right in front of her by the minute. Tourists rummaged through stacks of T-shirts with bold lettering spelling out Throw Me the Beads, NOLA, or Laissez les Bons Temps Rouler. *Well, I certainly agree with that philosophy*, Sadie thought to herself, knowing the well-known English equivalent "Let the Good Times Roll." Nothing could better describe her outlook on life: live large, life is short, enjoy with gusto.

Moving on, Sadie stopped next to a crowded food counter, baffled by a sign. "Gator on a stick?" she read aloud to no one in particular. She wasn't sure whether to be intrigued or terrified.

"Yes, ma'am," a twenty-something young man commented from the nearest counter seat. He wore a black-and-gold New Orleans Saints T-shirt with the phrase Who dat? in bold lettering. "You should try it. It's delicious. Can't beat fresh farmed gator." He waved a kebob-style stick in the air and took a bite of its skewered goods. "Want a taste?" He extended the stick toward Sadie and then pulled it back when she politely shook her head. Coco's head popped up from inside Sadie's bag but not quickly enough to sneak a bite. With a dramatic sigh, the Yorkie dropped back inside the tote.

"Maybe another time," Sadie said, fluffing her boa nonchalantly. "But thank you anyway," she added. She moved along the counter, intending to leave, but paused upon overhearing a remark that caught her attention.

"Did you read that article about the poor woman at a local bakery?" A woman serving food directed the question to a customer who was reading a newspaper at the counter. Sadie rummaged through her bag, a stalling tactic that resulted in an annoyed yip. At times Coco simply didn't want to be disturbed.

"I did," the customer said. "Things like that happen in cities like this."

Sadie glanced up and immediately dropped her gaze back toward her tote as the man looked her way. But the sneak peek was long enough to take stock of his appearance: middle-aged, casually dressed, hair overstyled, a bit out of place among the crowd. It struck her that both his speech and mannerisms seemed insensitive, considering the subject matter.

"What do you make of that, Coco?" Sadie said after she walked away. She received only silence in return, a sign she interpreted to be Coco's annoyance at being shuffled around in the tote bag, mixed with the failed attempt to sneak a bite of alligator.

A temptation to keep an eye on the man tugged at Sadie, but she thought better of it. She didn't really have any reason to, other than her own curiosity, and there were still plenty of vendor tables to explore. Maybe he was just the type not prone to showing reactions in public, or he simply didn't have a response at all.

"Look at this wonderful hand-painted pottery, Coco," Sadie said as they stopped by a booth with a variety of dishes. "We may need a set of mugs to take home with us." Coco, still annoyed, didn't respond.

An hour and several shopping splurges later, Sadie headed back to the hotel and spread her purchases out on the bedspread.

"Maybe I'll wear this to the wine-and-appetizer hour," she said, holding up a loose, Bohemian-style blouse in bright yellow and a set of hand-painted bangle bracelets.

She changed into the blouse and slid the bangles on one wrist, shaking her arm just to hear the sound they made.

Picking up a decorative mask with sequins around the edges, she admired the ribbons trailing below. "And this will look fabulous in the living room... or maybe the hallway."

Several bottles of hot sauce with exotic labels and varying degrees of heat completed the collection of purchases. Whether she'd be brave enough to try them all remained to be seen. But they'd look impressive on a kitchen shelf.

Coco had not been overlooked during the shopping spree either. Sadie had carefully chosen an infant T-shirt just the right size for the petite Yorkie. She set Coco on the bed and pulled the bright pink garment over the Yorkie's furry head and inserted each front leg in one armhole. With the front of the shirt on Coco's back, the catchy wording couldn't be missed.

"All right, my little *Voodoo Princess*," Sadie said. "Now that you're decked out too, we're ready for the hotel lobby. Let's go meet up with Clotile."

FIVE

The hotel lounge off the main lobby boasted an elegant spread of wine, crackers, and cheeses, as well as assorted appetizers and dips. A handful of guests gathered in conversation near the food while a few solo visitors sipped wine and browsed magazines independently.

Sadie poured herself a glass of pinot grigio, dipped a water cracker into a hot crawfish dip, and looked around. Seeing no sign of Clotile, she layered an ample selection of appetizers on a small plate, then took a seat on a chair near a front window. Within seconds, her foot began tapping to the light jazz music the hotel had floating through the room. Coco apparently enjoyed the musical selection, too, as Sadie felt rhythmic movement within her tote bag.

Sitting alone in a gathering always provided an opportunity to take in the surrounding environment, and Sadie wasn't about to let this chance go to waste. Just the events since her arrival were enough to make her curious, aside from the usual intrigue of people-watching. From her vantage point, nothing seemed noticeably different from any other hotel's wine-and-appetizer hour. Perhaps a murder a few blocks away wasn't enough to throw off the daily norm? Somehow, in spite of the calm appearance of the room, Sadie found that difficult to believe. She was well aware that appearances could be deceiving.

"There you are!"

Clotile's voice reached Sadie's ears just as she was biting into a spread of pimento cheese on crispy flatbread. Unable to answer with her mouth full, she waved Clotile over to the chair beside her, patting the seat. Clotile set a clutch purse and sweater down on the chair, fetched a plate of culinary goodies from the serving table, and returned to take a seat next to Sadie.

"Anything new?" Sadie asked.

Clotile shook her head while popping a stuffed mushroom into her mouth. "Nothing," she said after swallowing. "Lisette is home resting. The bakery is sealed off. Everything else seems like any other day." She eyed the selections on her plate, picked up a shrimp, and then paused. "Except..."

"Except what?" Sadie asked, eyebrows raised.

"Look at the hotel's front counter," Clotile said, nodding in that direction.

Sadie followed Clotile's head nod and took in the scene at the check-in desk. A few guests waiting for room keys, a housekeeper added water to a flower display, but nothing seemed out of place.

"What?" Sadie said. "Looks like everyday business to me."

"Yes," Clotile agreed, "other than Horace."

"Horace?"

"Horace LeBlanc," Clotile explained in a hushed voice.

Sadie recognized the last name immediately. "As in the Arnaud-LeBlanc rift?"

"Exactly," Clotile said. "Very odd."

"Why odd?" Sadie asked. "He's part owner, right?"

"Yes," Clotile said. "But he's never here. He doesn't even live here. He moved away years ago."

"Where did he move to?" Sadie asked.

"Miami, I think," Clotile said. "Or Chicago. Or Las Vegas.

Someplace like that. He moved shortly after the scandal broke out about the hotel." She shrugged her shoulders. "Can't say I blame him. Mimi was running the hotel anyway. Who likes being the center of nasty gossip?"

Clotile's question was clearly rhetorical, so Sadie simply asked the obvious, lowering her voice appropriately. "What scandal? What kind of gossip?" she whispered.

"They say he embezzled money." Clotile dipped a cold shrimp in Cajun-spiced cocktail sauce, took a bite, then set the tail on the edge of her plate before picking up another.

"Well, did he?" Sadie asked.

Clotile shrugged her shoulders. "They were never able to prove it. He insisted it had to be someone else. Police investigated both families since they both had access to the cash, as well as the bank account. They accused Mimi's father too. But he was cleared. So was Horace. Still, the families accused each other for years."

Sadie almost choked on a cracker smothered with hot crawfish dip. "Mimi? The woman who died at the bakery this morning? That seems like quite the coincidence, don't you think? That the daughter of the other man involved in the scandal happens to die just when…" She looked back at the hotel's front counter. "What is this man's name again? Horace?"

Clotile nodded.

"Just when Horace comes to town," Sadie said, finishing her statement. It was puzzling, and she could never resist a good puzzle. And, after all, she'd seen the poor woman die.

"You know, it might have just been a heart attack," Clotile said. "There's no way to know at this point."

Sadie mulled that over. "But then why the coughing fit that Mimi had before collapsing, and the dizziness, the trouble walking? Why not chest pains or arm discomfort or nausea? Those symptoms would make more sense at the onset of a heart attack."

"Maybe a stroke?" Clotile suggested.

Sadie started to make additional guesses but then stopped herself. She wasn't a doctor. It was ridiculous for her to analyze the scene that morning in the bakery even though she'd witnessed it with her own eyes. Her entire medical knowledge was based on her penchant for reading murder mysteries. That was hardly the equivalent of attending medical school. Maybe this was one situation she should stay out of.

"I'm sure there will be more information in the morning paper," Clotile said. "And I plan to go by Lisette's place later on to see how she's doing."

"I could come with you," Sadie said, immediately forgetting her thoughts from ten seconds before.

"I'll see if she feels up to company," Clotile said. "It's been such a shock; I'm not sure what sort of mood she'll be in."

"Of course," Sadie said. To call it a shock was an understatement. Seeing someone die was enough in itself, not to mention the effect on the business. Who knew how long the bakery would stay closed. And would customers even want to return when it opened?

Sadie excused herself momentarily, hooked her tote bag over her shoulder, and sauntered back to the appetizer table. Surveying a platter of petite hush puppies, she mulled over the future of Lisette's business. She glanced back at the hotel counter, observing a calm, hospitable interaction between Horace LeBlanc and a guest. Popping a hush puppy in her mouth, she piled a few on her plate, dropped one in her tote bag, and returned to her seat.

"I'm not certain Horace has anything to do with Mimi's

demise." Sadie spoke half to Clotile and half to herself.

"Well, we don't know if anyone had anything to do with it," Clotile said. "In fact, I doubt anyone did. It may very well have been natural. Mimi wasn't exactly a spring chicken."

Sadie frowned at that statement. Mimi had easily been a few years younger than herself.

"Still," Clotile continued, "it seems quite the coincidence that Horace appears just now. I'm sure if it turns out to be foul play the authorities will question him."

Sadie dropped another miniature hush puppy in her tote, earning a questioning look from Clotile, as well as a few nearby guests. Fortunately, the chatter of the crowd covered up the yip of *thank you* that followed.

"Think of the effect this will have on Lisette's business even if it's ruled an accident," Sadie pointed out. "Just the association with death could be enough to keep customers away."

"I don't know," Clotile said. "Lisette has a solid following. Her customers are devoted, if not addicts. I know I've been addicted to her pralines since the first time I had one.

"Yes, I can certainly understand that," Sadie said, remembering the mouthwatering concoction Clotile had offered her on the plane.

"Still, you may have a point," Clotile said pensively. "What exactly are you getting at?"

"Competition," Sadie said. "When a popular business suffers, the competition benefits. And you did say in your text that someone was looking out the window across the street."

Clotile eyed Sadie warily. "You read a lot of murder mysteries, don't you?"

"As a matter of fact, I do," Sadie said. "But that's beside the point. If you think that means my imagination is getting the better of me, it isn't. I'm just debating different possible theories and motives."

"For a murder that might not even have happened," Clotile said.

"Well, yes," Sadie admitted. "I suppose I'm getting ahead of things. It's all conjecture at this point, obviously."

Clotile finished the last shrimp on her plate and stood up. "I really should go see how Lisette is doing, as difficult as it is to pass up another round of appetizers."

"Understandable on both accounts," Sadie said. "I may stay for one more dab of that crawfish dip though. I'm debating it."

"Well, enjoy," Clotile said. "I can't blame you a bit. Besides, you're on vacation, right? That means no calories."

Sadie laughed. "Yes, that has always been my philosophy, hence the extra baggage." She patted one hip in explanation.

"You and me both," Clotile said, copying her gesture. "I'll let you know if I find out anything more." She started to leave but turned as Sadie called to her and waved her back.

"Just curious, what relation is the man at the front desk to the owner of that other bakery, the one across the street from Lisette's place?" Sadie asked.

Clotile looked across the room and then back at Sadie. She lowered her voice. "Horace?"

"Yes, Horace, the man you pointed out to me earlier," Sadie said. "You said he's a LeBlanc, the same as the family who owns the bakery across from Lisette's."

"Bluette's Beignets," Clotile clarified.

"Yes. Is he Bluette's father, by any chance?"

Clotile shook her head. "No. He's her uncle. Why?"

"I see," Sadie said, not seeing at all. She wasn't even sure why she'd asked the question. "No reason. Just seems like a complicated family."

"Sometimes I think all families are complicated," Clotile said, sighing.

Sadie nodded. "I suppose so." She watched Clotile leave and then stood, hoisting her tote bag over her shoulder. She disposed of her appetizer plate and headed back to her room, mulling over the conversation. *Yes, families are complicated. But perhaps not as complicated as those two.*

SIX

Sadie sat up in bed and leaned over to check the clock on the nightstand. At two a.m. in the morning, she should have been asleep yet was sure she'd heard sounds outside. As it was, she'd dozed off early with a copy of Agatha Christie's *Death on the Nile* on her lap. Having filled up on appetizers, she'd chosen to skip dinner, as tempting as another culinary adventure on Bourbon Street sounded. Instead, she'd browsed the hotel's guest library and borrowed the classic mystery novel for the evening. The hotel had kindly delivered complimentary hot chocolate to her room. Changing into a favorite pair of pajamas—bright purple with assorted farm animal faces—she'd snuggled up in bed to escape into a fictional Egyptian outing with Hercule Poirot while sipping the delicious beverage.

With a twist of the nightlight's knob, 40-watt illumination bathed the room in light. Coco let out a yip of disapproval at being roused from her beauty sleep. Sadie was certain she received a canine frown upon making eye contact with the Yorkie.

"I apologize, Coco," Sadie said. "But sometimes you just can't get a good night's sleep even if you try." Coco yawned and dropped her head back down on the velvet pillow in her travel palace, determined to try. "Fine," Sadie said. "Go ahead and sleep. But I'm going out to see what's going on. I'm sure I heard an odd noise."

Wrapping the hotel's luxurious logoed bathrobe around her, she slid her feet into her favorite leopard-print slippers and stepped outside to explore. The outdoor hallway faced a lovely interior courtyard. Soft garden lights lit flowering bushes from ground level, adding an enchanted feeling to the peaceful, deserted exterior. No lights shone from other rooms' windows. Perhaps she'd imagined a noise? Or dreamed it?

Turning back toward her door, she paused at the sound of voices. Too far away to decipher what they were saying, Sadie followed the sound until it grew louder, arriving at the back gate, where a conversation was taking place on the other side. She hunched down and pressed one ear against the gate in order to listen.

"You shouldn't have come here," a man's voice said. Unrecognizable, it clearly belonged to someone who was upset. It almost had a hissing tone to it.

"It's none of your business whether I'm here or not," another voice said, also male, yet calmer than the first. "If anyone belongs here, it's me."

Sadie shifted her position as her knees began to ache, careful to remain silent.

"I'm making it my business now," the first voice insisted. "It doesn't look good for you to be around now. There's too much at stake."

"You may be used to pushing people around, but you're wasting your time," the other man said. "You don't scare me."

"Quite naïve of you…" Much to Sadie's frustration, this statement seemed to be followed by a name, but it was too mumbled to make out.

One of the men coughed, and the other hushed him up. A shuffling of feet followed, and the sounds moved farther and farther away until they disappeared completely. Sadie tiptoed back to her room, where she was greeted again by an annoyed Coco, who had fallen back to sleep while Sadie was outside.

"There were two men out in back, Coco," Sadie said, completely aware that Coco had no interest in listening. Still, conversations with the Yorkie, although one-sided, had proven useful to Sadie in the past. In truth, there were clear advantages to having discussions with someone who couldn't talk back.

Coco stretched out on her velvet pillow and rolled over onto her back, front paws extended in the air like antennae. She closed her eyes.

"One man sounded threatening," Sadie continued, not caring in the least that Coco wasn't responding. She removed the hotel robe and hung it back up on a hook and continued. "The other didn't seem intimidated. He stood his ground. If only I knew what that ground was." She set her slippers beside the bed and climbed back under the covers.

Coco let out a soft snore, drawing Sadie's attention away from the ceiling. "I know," she said to the sleeping bundle of fur. "Exactly what I was just thinking: I wish I'd heard Horace's voice today. I might have been able to recognize it tonight—*if* he was one of the two men in the back alley, of course, which I have no way of knowing."

Sadie was just pondering that thought when she heard a slight creak coming from the direction of the alley. *The gate?* Reaching over, she quickly clicked off the light on the nightstand, letting the room fall into darkness just as she heard the sound of the gate latching. If one of the men from the alley was going to walk through the courtyard, it would be best if she didn't appear to be awake. Even as nonspecific as the spoken words were, she didn't want the men to suspect she'd overheard them.

The exterior lights formed a soft backdrop to the garden courtyard outside, especially with her room lights now completely off. She was suddenly thankful that she hadn't thought to pull the heavier set of curtains closed, as the wispy interior curtain allowed her to make out a shadow passing by her window. Was it a man's shadow? She wasn't sure, but it only made sense, having overheard the conversation before.

Suddenly Coco yipped in her sleep, causing the shadow to pause outside her window. *Not now, Coco! Not one of your silly dreams about chasing chipmunks!* Sadie was used to the petite canine's habit of talking in her sleep, but this was not the time. Remaining still, Sadie held her breath and waited until the shadow moved on, and then exhaled, relieved. There were no more sounds after that, and after some effort, she finally fell back asleep.

* * *

The local paper was the first thing to catch Sadie's eye when she entered the lobby the following morning, even before her sight landed on the goal of her usual morning search—a pot of fresh coffee. She lifted the newspaper casually off the sofa, where it had been left by another guest. Tucking it under her arm, she poured herself a cup of coffee and took a seat in a wing-backed chair near a sunny front window of the lobby. She set her coffee down and thumbed through the paper until she found a small article on the fifth page. It barely read as an obituary, lacking the usual details of a person's life. It simply said that Mimi Arnaud had died unexpectedly the morning before at Chez Lisette Patisserie.

Well, there you have it, Sadie thought. There *is* such a thing as bad publicity. She felt a pang of sympathy for

Lisette. No business owner wanted a death linked with the business name.

Have you seen the paper yet? The text from Clotile came through just as Sadie set the newspaper aside.

Yes. Just read it. Sadie sent the text back. She eyed her phone strangely, as if it were asking her to type more. But what else was there to say? There was nothing unexpected in the article. It was so brief it could hardly even be called an article.

I'm at Bluette's. Clotile's text surprised Sadie, though she couldn't pinpoint why. If a person's favorite morning haunt was closed, it seemed natural to head to another. Why not the nearest one?

Crowded? Sadie typed the text and hit Send.

Packed, with a line outside. Again, Clotile's text took Sadie by surprise, and she still wasn't sure why. Perhaps she felt sorry for Lisette, knowing some of that business would normally be hers. Or was it that Clotile's morning report confirmed one of her theories: a competitive business would benefit from the misfortune of another. Naturally, this would give the competitor a motive for causing said misfortune.

"I don't know, Coco," Sadie said aloud. Coco stuck her head out of the tote and yipped at the sound of her name. "Yes, I agree. It seems extreme. But then again…" Her voice trailed off as she saw Horace LeBlanc step out of a side door behind the front desk. He scribbled something on a piece of paper, folded it neatly, and slipped it into his shirt pocket. He then stepped away and disappeared into a back office.

Sadie thought back to the night before, remembering the voices she'd overheard in the back alley. Standing, she set her coffee aside and walked to the front desk. A moment later, Horace LeBlanc was standing in front of her.

"Good morning," he said, greeting Sadie in a somber yet professional manner.

Two words, Sadie thought. *Not enough.*

"How may I help you?" *Better, but still not quite...*

"May I help you with something?" Horace LeBlanc's forehead furrowed, causing Sadie to realize she had yet to respond to anything the man had said.

"Oh! I'm so sorry!" Sadie exclaimed. "Not enough coffee yet, I guess."

"We have coffee set up across the room, in the lobby area," Horace said. "Help yourself."

"Thank you," Sadie said, turning away from the counter.

"Ma'am, did you have a question?"

Sadie turned back and smiled politely. "You answered my question, thank you."

"My pleasure," Horace said. "If there's anything else we can do to make your stay pleasant, don't hesitate to ask. We're here to help."

Sadie smiled. Now she'd struck gold. Twenty-two words, not even counting contractions and extra syllables. It was just enough to confirm what she suspected. Horace LeBlanc had been one of the men in the alley the night before. Yet questions remained. Why was he there? And did he have anything to do with Mimi Arnaud's demise?

SEVEN

Clotile had not been exaggerating. Not only was the interior of Bluette's Beignets filled to capacity, the line stretched down the block. A podium-type sign stood near the front door, attractively scrolled lettering announcing Please wait to be seated. Sadie didn't remember seeing anything of the sort the day before.

As she had the previous morning, she'd walked over from the hotel. This time, rather than keep Coco in her tote bag as she usually did, she attached a rhinestone-studded leash that matched the Yorkie's collar. She always suspected Coco felt snubbed to be on a leash but tolerated it in exchange for being able to strut around and show herself off to others. Coco had never been shy. If anything, she was always curious about exploring her surroundings. On the other hand, she never complained about being chauffeured in Sadie's tote bag either. Perhaps the velvet lining and custom iPod system had something to do with it.

Sadie stood across from Bluette's, yet not directly in front of Lisette's taped-off storefront, which somehow felt disrespectful as well as blatantly obvious to those in line across the street. But she could see the commotion easily from where she stood. And the fresh-baked aromas were not beyond her either, nor did they escape Coco's attention. The Yorkie's nose was twitching and sniffing like someone with a frequent nervous tic.

"Don't get your hopes up, Coco," Sadie warned. "I'm not waiting in a line like that for anyone, not even you." Coco pawed the ground, whether at frustration over Sadie's comment or simply to bat her own shadow, a habit on occasion.

Two police officers emerged from Bluette's Beignets, to-go bag in hand. They crossed the street, nodded politely to Sadie, and ducked inside Lisette's place. One stepped back out almost immediately.

"Can I help you with something? I'm Detective Broussard. I'm in charge of the investigation here. I couldn't help but notice you were standing nearby." The officer paused and glanced across the street. "I'm afraid you'll need to go over there if you're looking for baked goods. This one is closed today, due to an incident yesterday."

"I know," Sadie said, nodding. "I was here when it happened."

The detective paused, taking in Sadie, the rhinestone leash, and the sniffing dog on the end of the sparkling rope. "You were here?"

Sadie nodded. "Yes, I'm afraid so. Not that I would have chosen to be. It was fairly dramatic and certainly unsettling."

"I can imagine," Detective Broussard said. "Why don't you come inside? Maybe you could shed some light on the events?"

Sadie looked down at Coco, who was still eyeing Bluette's Beignets with longing, nose sniffing. "Well, I...," Sadie began.

"Don't worry," the detective said, "you can bring it in."

"Her," Sadie said with a touch of indignation. Not that the detective had any way to tell from a distance, but Coco still deserved the proper designation.

"You can bring *her* in," Detective Broussard said, correcting his statement. "The health codes won't matter today, as there's nothing in there that anyone will be able to sell, plus the place will be wiped clean after we finish inspecting everything."

"Yes," Sadie said. "I imagine that's the only way it would be able to reopen."

"Exactly," the detective said. He opened the front door and held up a yellow tape that blocked the entrance. Sadie approached and entered the building, a reluctant Coco behind her, head swiveling and nose still sniffing in the opposite direction.

Once inside, Sadie looked around the interior. Lisette's bakery held none of the charm it had the previous morning. With the lights off and the tables empty, it felt not only deserted but ominous. How much of this atmosphere was the dim lighting or the knowledge of what had happened the day before, Sadie wasn't sure. But something felt off about the place.

"Why the police tape across the door?" Sadie asked suddenly. "Isn't that only used for a crime scene? Have you determined this was a crime?" The thought had occurred to her, especially with the odd happenings at the hotel, but nothing official or even speculative had been in the paper that morning.

The detective cleared his throat and coughed, as if the question took him by surprise and he needed to gather his thoughts before answering. Sadie suddenly had a flash of déjà vu and hoped the cough wasn't about to lead to a repeat performance of the morning before.

"We don't know that it is a crime scene," Detective Broussard said. "But we also don't know that it isn't. We're trying to rule out possibilities."

"Because of the Arnaud-LeBlanc feud?" Sadie asked, letting her curiosity get the better of the wiser decision to stay uninvolved.

Detective Broussard blinked. "Are you from around here?" he asked, eyeing Sadie's appearance dubiously. Clearly, her orange blouse with vertical seashell designs along the button-down front didn't shout *New Orleans local.*

"No," Sadie said. "I'm visiting from San Francisco."

"Ah." The detective nodded his head as if that explained something. "A Californian." And there it was, the insinuation she often encountered when traveling. *We're not a different species, you know,* Sadie said to herself. Then, as a matter of pride, she raised one eyebrow and repeated the statement aloud.

"Of course not," Detective Broussard said, his tone more of courtesy than agreement.

"Well, now that we cleared that up," Sadie said, "tell me what you'd like to know." She took a seat at the nearest table, looped Coco's leash around the chair leg, and folded her hands on the table, prepared for what now was beginning to feel like an interrogation. The feeling was mildly discomforting.

"Where were you in relation to Ms. Arnaud's table?"

Sadie nodded toward the table she and Clotile had occupied. "We were at that table over there, near the wall."

"We?" the detective repeated.

"Yes, I met a friend of Lisette's on the flight here, Clotile. She told me about the bakery and invited me to meet her for breakfast. I'm glad she did too. The croissants are delicious. I was going to take home a raspberry-almond tart, but… well, I thought better of it after what happened."

"I see. So you don't know Lisette personally."

"No. I met her, but it was far too busy to socialize."

The detective glanced out the front window. "As busy as the place across the street?"

Sadie shook her head. "I wouldn't say that. It was busy inside, but there wasn't a line of customers waiting to get in.

"What about across the street? Did you see a line there?"

Sadie thought back. She hadn't noticed a line at either bakery, at least not that she could remember. She hadn't really paid attention to Bluette's Beignets. "No."

"So there's more business there this morning than yesterday," the detective said.

"Well, yes," Sadie said. "But that's to be expected with this bakery closed. I'm sure there are customers in line there who came here, only to find it closed." She paused. "Wait, that's exactly what you're getting at, isn't it? You *do* think this was a crime."

"I'm not saying that," the detective said. "I'm merely asking what you observed."

Sadie nodded, understanding all too well in spite of the spoken words. "It's possible to say things without saying them, you know."

"Hey, Broussard!" The male voice shouting from the back of the bakery startled Sadie, who had forgotten by now that two detectives had entered the building, not one. "Better get back here. We have a problem—a very small problem."

"Well, if it's a 'very small problem,' it can wait." Detective Broussard turned back to Sadie, ready to ask more questions.

"I don't suggest that," the other detective called out.

Detective Broussard sighed visibly and stuffed his notebook back in his pocket. "I'll be right back," he said to Sadie. He walked to the back and disappeared for a moment but then called back to Sadie. "Ma'am, I think you'd better come back here."

"Well," Sadie said. "What do you know, Coco? We have an excuse to look around, with the detective's blessing. I'll be right back." She lowered her hand to pat Coco on the head, fumbling around in an attempt to find the furry canine. Suddenly overcome with a sinking sensation, she looked down, only to find no sign of the dog or rhinestone leash. *This can't be good,* she muttered to herself.

"Now," Broussard called.

"On my way," Sadie answered, keeping her voice light in spite of the dreaded scene she anticipated. She rushed to the back, stepped behind the counter and into the kitchen, where she found Coco sitting in the middle of a large center island, covered with flour. Rhinestones on the leash sparkled faintly underneath a matching layer of white. Seeing Sadie, Coco stood up and shook her body, sending a mist of white powder in all directions, and then trotted to the edge of the counter. With a happy leap, she landed in Sadie's arms.

"Coco!" Sadie reprimanded the Yorkie, though fought back a smile at the same time. Coco looked up at her with an expression of innocence that melted Sadie's heart in spite of the awkward situation. "What have you done?"

"I can tell you what it's done," the second detective said, glaring at Sadie. "Contaminated evidence, that's what."

"*She,*" Sadie corrected. "*She* contaminated evidence." She paused. "Wait, you're saying this is evidence?"

"We're not saying…" Broussard shot a look at his partner.

"I know, I know," Sadie said. "You're not saying anything. But you're thinking…" She froze suddenly, looking down at Coco with a panicked expression. "Oh dear!" Turning, she raced out of the kitchen and straight to the front door.

"We still need…," Detective Broussard called after her.

"I don't care what you need," Sadie shouted in return. "I need a veterinarian. And I need one right now!"

EIGHT

The veterinarian, a soft-spoken man by the name of Dr. Perault, placed Coco on the examination table and gently pressed the Yorkie's abdomen and then the hindquarters and then each leg. He looked in each petite eye, in both pointed ears, and inside the dog's tiny mouth. Standing back, he brushed his hands together, sending puffs of white powder into the air. "She's fine," he said, looking at Sadie curiously.

"Are you sure?" Sadie said. Her worried expression echoed her fears. Perault's Peterinary Clinic had been the closest animal hospital she could find. There hadn't been time to check recommendations or reviews.

"Yes," the doctor said. "There's nothing wrong with your dog, at least nothing that a good bath wouldn't take care of."

"I see," Sadie said, relieved to hear Coco was all right yet somewhat insulted at the reference to a bath. After all, Coco was likely the most spoiled canine in all of San Francisco. She had an expensive, highly recommended groomer, a mani-pedi professional for her paws, and her own personal masseuse. Still, Sadie had to admit Coco's appearance on this particular day was not up to par.

"Why don't you tell me again what happened," Dr. Perault said.

Sadie inhaled and exhaled. She'd been in such a panic to have Coco seen by the vet that she hadn't explained the traumatic event itself. "She fell into a barrel of flour, apparently."

"I see. Well, that does explain her appearance." The vet brushed his hands against his white coat, causing another flutter of powder to drift outward. "But it doesn't explain why you were so panic-stricken. My receptionist said you almost jumped over the desk." He lowered his eyes briefly and then had the good manners to look back up immediately. Sadie was certain the image of her plump body plummeting over the front counter was nothing short of horrifying.

"This happened at Chez Lisette Patisserie," Sadie said, certain this would explain everything. "In the kitchen, today," she added when she didn't get a response. "You know there was a death there yesterday, right?" She tapped one foot, impatient. Didn't veterinarians read newspapers?

"Yes, I heard about that on the news," Dr. Perault said. He glanced at his watch and then looked back up. "But I don't see the connection with your dog's condition—or lack thereof, I should say."

"The connection is the flour," Sadie said. "It's the same flour that might have been used to make the raspberry-almond tart."

Dr. Perault tilted his head and gave Sadie an odd look. She couldn't determine if he was beginning to understand or if he simply thought she was crazy. Perhaps it was some of each.

"The raspberry-almond tart?"

"The one that Mimi Arnaud's head fell into when she died," Sadie blurted out. "I watched it happen myself. I was at the bakery. She was acting out of sorts, and then her head simply slammed into the tart—the tart made with the flour you now see on my dog. Or so I assume since that's what's in the kitchen. The detectives are still investigating the crime scene."

"The crime scene?"

Now Sadie knew she had his attention but not in the way she wanted. It wasn't officially a crime scene, so there was no excuse for her calling it that. On the other hand, the detectives hadn't specifically said it wasn't. Still, she should have known better than to phrase it that way.

"I thought the woman died a natural death. It didn't say anything different in the newspaper," Dr. Perault said.

Aha, Sadie thought. *They do read newspapers!* "Well, they don't know, I guess. That's why the detectives are there this morning, investigating. And we were there helping."

"I can see that now," Dr. Perault said, looking at the flour-covered Yorkie. "I really don't think you have anything to be concerned about. This is simply a case of a dog getting into mischief. There's no health problem here that I can see. Does she do this type of thing often?"

"Constantly," Sadie admitted.

The doctor smiled. "Then my diagnosis is that you have a terrier."

A knock on the exam room door preceded an interruption by the front desk receptionist. "Dr. Perrault, Mrs. Martin is here with Rufus again. He swallowed a pair of argyle socks."

"Again?"

"Apparently. How long should I tell her the wait will be?" The receptionist gave Sadie an apologetic look.

"Just put them in Exam Room 2, and I'll be right there." The vet turned back to Sadie as the door closed. "I truly believe your dog is fine. But I will touch base with the detectives to make sure there's nothing to be concerned about. Meanwhile, I prescribe a bath for Coco here and perhaps a glass of wine for you, to help you relax."

Sadie sighed. The idea of a glass of wine did sound appealing, and she couldn't argue about Coco needing a bath.

* * *

"But you must have a pet-grooming salon somewhere around here."

Sadie leaned against the hotel's front desk, a dusty Coco dangling between her chest and one arm. She'd considered putting the Yorkie back in the tote bag after returning to the hotel but figured she'd then have to find a way to do laundry too. It would be enough just trying to get the dog cleaned up.

The clerk at the front desk, a college-aged girl she hadn't seen working there before, pulled a map from below the counter and pointed to an area a good two miles away. "I'm sorry, Ms. Kramer, but this is the closest one I know of. I'll be happy to give them a call for you, to see if they have an opening."

Sadie debated this but hesitated at the distance. "I don't have a car…"

Predictably, the clerk offered to call a taxi.

"That's all right," Sadie said. "Thank you for offering. I'll just take the map with me if you don't mind. Maybe I'll give them a call in a bit." She lifted the map with her free hand, thanked the girl again for offering help, and walked away, leaving the young clerk wiping flour off the front counter.

Back in the hotel room, Sadie set Coco down on the tiled bathroom floor and contemplated the predicament. In spite of all the flour Coco had shed during the day, she still had a solid coat of it in her fur. Sadie looked in the mirror, noting that she had much the same look.

"I guess we're in this together now. I must look as dusty as you do." Sadie eyed Coco, who simply licked her paw and then sputtered in disgust.

"Tastes as bad as it looks, huh?" Sadie said. "Maybe you'll think twice before you go gallivanting around a kitchen full of baking ingredients."

Sadie turned to the mirror, a closer look confirming her suspicions. Her face was veiled in a thin coat of powder, similar to what her mother used to blot on with a gigantic—at least it seemed gigantic to her as a child—pink puff. Her arms matched her face, and her blouse's seashell design trim looked as if it had spent the day on a sandy beach.

There was only one easy solution to the combination of problems that Sadie could think of. She looked at the claw-foot tub with a fleur-de-lis-patterned shower curtain hanging around it and then looked back at Coco. The Yorkie returned her look with suspicion. Taking a deep breath, Sadie reached behind the shower curtain and turned the water on.

NINE

S unny and welcoming, the courtyard outside the hotel room seemed the most inviting place to dry off after a mother-doggie water escapade. The warmth of the afternoon rays would serve to dry both hair and fur. A hairdryer was provided in the room, along with the many other amenities the hotel offered to each guest. But the lure of the sunny courtyard appealed to Sadie, so she donned a colorful muumuu and settled in on a bench next to a flowing fountain. She leaned back and closed her eyes.

"Lovely, that sound of babbling water, don't you think?"

Sadie's eyes popped open. She hadn't heard anyone approach, and the sight of Horace LeBlanc replaced her momentary relaxation with a nervous shiver. Was he already in the courtyard and she just hadn't seen him? Or had he seen her enter the courtyard and chosen to follow? And if so, why?

"Yes," Sadie said as she pulled Coco a little closer, protectively. "I find it relaxing." *Usually*, she added to herself.

"I wondered if you might have any other questions. It seemed you did when you asked about the coffee this morning." The man took a seat next to Sadie, who tried to stifle an urge to shudder.

"I can't think of anything I'd like to ask at the moment," Sadie said. *Except maybe what you were doing in the alley last night...*

"I see," Horace said, standing up as abruptly as he'd taken

a seat. He smoothed his suit jacket with his hands, glanced around, and then turned to face Sadie. "Well, that's fine then. Just feel free to ask at the front desk if there's anything you need. We do like our guest experience to be perfect."

Sadie nodded. "Thank you, I will." She mustered a smile that she hoped looked sincere and then watched him walk away.

"That's very odd," Sadie said, directing her comment to Coco. "In fact, it's not very odd, it's *extremely* odd."

Coco tilted her head sideways and stared at Sadie, and then responded by licking one paw.

"I agree," Sadie said as if Coco had answered her verbally. "If I'd had other questions, I would have asked him earlier."

A text from Clotile interrupted Sadie's thoughts.

The police are taking Julien in for questioning!

"Coco!" Sadie whispered to the Yorkie. "The police are questioning Julien. What do you think about that?" She then sent a text back to Clotile.

Who's Julien?

Sadie glanced around to make sure Horace LeBlanc hadn't decided to slink back into the courtyard. She already had a sneaking suspicion that he had something to do with Mimi Arnaud's murder, though she didn't have anything more to go on than the creepy feeling she had when he was around.

The pastry chef. Didn't I tell you this before? Julien Simon is Lisette's pastry chef.

"Looks like it might be the pastry chef," Sadie whispered to Coco, who simply yawned.

That's terrible! Sadie typed in return. *Do you think he's guilty?*

Sadie looked around the courtyard, mulling that over while waiting for Clotile's response. It seemed only normal that the pastry chef would be suspect. But why the delay in arresting him. Hadn't he been there the day Mimi Arnaud died?

He could be. He had access to the ingredients.

That made sense, of course, Sadie thought. He could have pulled something off without anyone noticing. She sent a text back to Clotile.

He might have slipped poison in that day. Just to Mimi's tart. When she came in.

Clotile's response was fast.

But he wasn't there that day.

Ah, hence the delay in the police questioning him, Sadie thought. If he'd been there at the time, surely the police would have detained him then. After all, they had questioned everyone in the building at the time.

Did they find evidence? Sadie typed.

Don't know. Lisette just sent me a text. No details.

"Why wouldn't he have been there that morning?" Sadie asked Coco. She tried to think of the reason for his absence. Maybe he was trying to cover his tracks by being out that day. In that case, he would have had to set someone else up. But how? How could anyone coordinate something like that without actually being there to see it through? An accomplice, perhaps?

Meeting Lisette for dinner. Join us?

Sadie wasn't about to turn down food, much less a chance to find out more about the pastry chef and his possible involvement.

Sure. When and where?

"We're going out to dinner," Sadie informed Coco, who merely scratched her chin.

CCCC 6:30.

Sadie looked at her phone as if tasked with detective work just to get dinner directions. She'd seen a lot of acronyms floating around in the texting universe, but this was a new one.

Oops, sorry. Cyril's Crazy Cajun Cookery. Close to you.

Sadie had an idea where it was. She'd passed it the first night.

See you there.

TEN

Cyril's Crazy Cajun Cookery was everything the name implied. It was owned by one Cyril Cragmont, it featured Cajun cooking that smelled divine, and it boasted an atmosphere that was nothing short of insane.

Sadie stepped through the front door of the Bourbon Street eatery into a blast of zydeco music. A male accordion player—Sadie estimated him to be in his fifties—accompanied several other musicians: one on guitar, another on drums, and yet another on... Sadie paused. Was that a washboard? Reminiscent of rhythm and blues, the music had a livelier beat. Sadie felt her tote bag start to bounce against her side, which didn't surprise her in the least. Coco had a passion for salsa, and this had a similar energy.

In spite of overhead lighting, the restaurant was dimly lit. Neon signs on the wall cast mysterious rainbow beams across the room, bouncing off spritzers and spectacles alike. Just about every shiny object in the crowded space seemed to glow. In a rare moment for Sadie, she suddenly felt conservatively dressed in her bright green tunic and paisley-print slacks. Had she known what to expect, she might have added one of the feather boas from the French Market. Maybe even two.

As her eyes adjusted to the low light, she spotted Clotile waving to her from a table near the band. Lisette sat alongside her, hand tapping on the table's surface, attention on the musicians. She nudged her way through the crowd and joined the two women.

"My, what a wild scene!" Sadie said, looking around with a pleased expression.

Clotile leaned closer, cupped her hand next to her mouth, and raised her voice. "What did you say?" She moved her hand to her ear, waiting for Sadie to answer.

"Great place!" Sadie shouted. Both Clotile and Lisette nodded in agreement. "Is it always this busy?" Again, both women nodded.

Lisette reached across the table and lifted a menu from a wire rack in the center of the table. She handed it to Sadie and pointed to various areas on the laminated sheet. "I highly recommend the jambalaya," she shouted. "It's Cyril's signature dish. But the oysters are excellent too." In spite of Lisette's attempt to offer suggestions, Sadie only caught a few words. With "jambalaya" being one of those, she pointed to the selection and nodded her head in approval.

A young woman in her midtwenties approached just as the band wound a tune down to an enthusiastic round of whoops and cheers. She wore skintight jeans and a clingy T-shirt with glittery letters spelling out Belle of the Boil. A crawfish illustration accompanied the wording. "What can I get you ladies?" the server asked, taking advantage of the break in music.

"Our visiting friend here would like the jambalaya," Clotile said, indicating Sadie. "I'll have an order of chargrilled oysters."

Lisette leaned toward the server and raised her voice as the band started into another tune. "I'll have a grilled catfish po-boy. Wait, make that fried. Please."

"Yours is on the house, Ms. Lisette," the young woman said. "We all feel terrible about what happened at your bakery. Cyril's going through withdrawal over your pralines."

"That's very kind but not necessary," Lisette insisted. "And you tell Cyril I'll be glad to whip up a batch of pralines at home for him."

"I'll tell him," the server said. She smiled and moved on to take an order at another table.

Clotile tapped Lisette on the arm to get her attention. The music was in full swing again, the accordion player belting out lyrics about someone stealing his chicken. Sadie could feel her tote bag bouncing along with the music.

"We want some pralines too," Clotile shouted, pointing to both Sadie and herself. Lisette grinned. Whether she had heard Clotile's words or not over the noise, she understood the request. It seemed to lift her spirits to hear the demand for her bakery goods.

Several tunes later, the abundant platters of food arrived. Conveniently, the band paused to take a break, which allowed the three women to finally converse with ease.

"Any news from the detectives?" Clotile asked as she popped an oyster in her mouth.

Lisette glanced briefly between Clotile and Sadie. She took a bite of her po-boy before responding, as if weighing what to say before speaking.

"Don't worry," Clotile said. "I've kept Sadie informed. You know the detectives questioned her too."

"Yes," Lisette said once her mouth was clear. "Sadie, I'm sorry you ended up in the middle of all this. You came to New Orleans for a vacation, not to get tangled up in a police investigation."

Sadie chuckled, thinking of a few past trips gone awry. "Don't worry. I seem to fall into these kinds of situations unexpectedly."

"Any update on Julien?" Clotile asked.

Lisette shook her head. "All I know is that they took him in for questioning. But I can't believe he'd be involved. I've known Julien for years. He's a big part of the reason the bakery has done well. And he loves the place, is very dedicated."

"Did he have any connection to Mimi Arnaud?" Sadie asked. She broke off a piece of french bread and dropped it into her tote bag. The tote calmed down momentarily, in spite of the lively music.

"No," Lisette said. "Not that I know of. I don't know Julien outside of work, but I'm sure he would have mentioned Mimi at some point or at least mentioned the family."

"He also wasn't there at the time," Sadie pointed out. "The detectives questioned all of us, including your staff."

"Right," Lisette said. "He'd already left for the morning. So it makes sense they'd question him at another time."

"Isn't that unusual?" Sadie asked. "That your pastry chef wouldn't be there? I mean, you serve pastry." Her tote bag began to bounce again as the band launched into another lively song.

Lisette shook her head. "No, it's not unusual at all. Julien starts baking very early in the morning, not long after midnight, in fact. He leaves around the time the café opens. We see each other for a few minutes to exchange any information pertaining to the day—a menu item that will be out of stock, for example, or special orders that are ready to be picked up."

"You really depend on him," Clotile said sympathetically. "How will you be able to reopen without him?" She cast an odd glance at Sadie's tote bag and then turned her attention back to Lisette.

"Why would I need to?" Lisette suddenly turned pale. "He can't possibly have anything to do with this! I'm sure they'll question him and let him go. At least I certainly hope so!"

"You say he's the one who sets up the special orders for pickup?" Sadie asked.

"Yes," Lisette said. "Customers order ahead of time or send in orders over the internet. Julian makes sure they're ready and labeled with the correct name of the person who ordered.

"Does that just apply to to-go orders?" Sadie asked.

"Mostly," Lisette said. "Occasionally a customer who is planning to dine in asks to have something set aside."

"Like Mimi Arnaud?" Sadie posed the question lightly. A possible chain of events was coming together in her mind, and she wanted to tread carefully.

"Well, yes," Lisette said. "But we already know who our regular customers will be and what they'll request. They don't have to order. We just make sure to set aside what they'll be asking for."

"Out of the main offerings in the case then. Set aside," Sadie said. She took a hearty bite of jambalaya and savored the spicy flavor.

"Yes, exactly," Lisette said. "It keeps our regulars happy to know they'll have their favorite item available."

"You're going somewhere with this, Sadie, aren't you?" Clotile asked.

Sadie nodded as she swallowed and set her fork down.

"Mimi Arnaud's serving of raspberry-almond tart was set aside in advance then, as a special order," Sadie said. "It wasn't pulled from inside the case like the tarts other customers were ordering."

"Right," Lisette said.

"That means her name was on that particular tart."

"Yes," Lisette said. "That's how we know it won't be given away." She paused. "Are you saying you think Julien is guilty because he's the one who separates the special orders?"

"Really, Sadie," Clotile said. "Is that what you're saying? That Julian had something to do with this?"

Sadie shook her head. "No, if anything, it might clear him. Reasonable doubt, you know."

Clotile and Lisette exchanged glances, confused. "I guess we don't understand what you're getting at," Clotile said.

"It's actually very simple," Sadie said. "Julien prepares the baked goods, looks over the orders, sets aside those that need to be on hold for specific customers, labels them, and then stocks the front shelves for regular customers. Then he leaves, done with his work for the day."

"Exactly," Lisette said. "That has always been our practice."

"And the special orders are kept where? Near the front counter?"

Lisette nodded. "Yes, so they are easy to reach when customers come to pick them up or dine in, whatever the case may be."

"This is within view of the public, right?" Sadie asked.

"Yes," Lisette said.

"Oh!" Clotile shouted loud enough that even a band member glanced her way. "I understand what Sadie's saying, Lisette. Anyone who knew where those orders were set aside could have tampered with the one for Mimi since her name was on it. So there's reasonable doubt that Julien is to blame. It also explains why no one else became ill."

"And that I could have taken tarts to go after all," Sadie mused.

"Better safe than sorry," Clotile pointed out.

"True," Sadie agreed. "So there's just one obvious question now."

"Which is?" Both Clotile and Lisette spoke at once.

"Who else had access to the special orders that morning

after Julien left?"

Both Sadie and Clotile looked to Lisette for an answer.

"Well, anyone on the staff," Lisette said. "And delivery people."

"Delivery people? How would they have access? Don't they have to come by appointment?" Sadie had little knowledge of the inner workings of eating establishments.

Lisette shook her head. "Not usually. Many deliveries are just regular orders. I adjust them by phone at the end of the day if we'll need different quantities the following day. And it gets busy when we open. It's not uncommon for the back door to be unlocked so that deliveries can be left inside without interrupting the activity."

"So anyone could have walked in the back," Sadie said. "Even someone who wasn't delivering supplies."

"I suppose so," Lisette said. "This is a patisserie, not a bank. We've never had to worry about tight security."

"That makes it hard to know who could have done it," Clotile said.

"Yes." Lisette sighed. "It certainly does."

ELEVEN

Sunshine filtered through the window of Sadie's hotel room, hinting at a perfect New Orleans morning. Sadie sat up, stretched, and debated plans for the day. Perhaps she'd go back to the French Market and look for a local artist's painting that would add some vibrant color to her San Francisco penthouse. Or she could head over to Jackson Square or St. Louis Cathedral or any number of other famous NOLA landmarks.

"What do you say, Coco? Should we go exploring today?"

Sadie dressed quickly, took Coco for a quick morning walk, passing through the lobby on her way back. Not yet caffeinated enough to endure small talk, she was relieved to see the front desk clerks busy with guest check-outs. She poured a cup to go and slipped out undisturbed.

Just before reentering her room, she noticed a police car pass slowly through the alley. Determined to stay away from drama for the day, she fought off her usual curiosity and settled into her accommodation's front parlor, Coco curled up by her feet.

"I suppose they're just doing a standard patrol of the alley," Sadie said to Coco. She then took a sip of coffee and set the cup on a side table. "Or... do you think they're coming to question Horace LeBlanc? It does seem strange that he's suddenly shown up in town just when Mimi Arnaud dies. Not to mention what an odd man he is. Creepy, I dare say."

A knock at the door interrupted Sadie's second sip of coffee.

"It must be housekeeping. So much for our uninterrupted morning, Coco. They should know this room isn't ready for service this early." Tsk-tsking the interruption, Sadie opened the door, surprised to find Detective Broussard outside, accompanied by two other policemen.

"Good morning, Detective…" Sadie tried to remember the detective's last name from her previous encounter with him at Chez Lisette Patisserie.

"Broussard," the detective said.

"Yes, Detective Broussard. What can I do for you?"

"We're here to search your room, Ms. Kramer." The detective's voice was stern and formal, yet polite.

"Whatever for?" Sadie said, shocked. "And… and," she stammered, "don't you need a warrant for that?"

To Sadie's dismay, Detective Broussard pulled a folded sheet of paper from his jacket pocket and held it up in the air. Stunned, she stepped back from the doorway to let the men enter.

"I absolutely don't understand," Sadie said, scooping Coco into her arms protectively. "I'm simply here on vacation. How did I manage to get mixed up in all this?"

"That's exactly what we're trying to figure out," Broussard said.

"I don't even know any of those people," Sadie insisted. "I didn't know a single person in this big *not-so-easy* city of yours before I arrived."

Broussard looked at Sadie and frowned. "Being defensive will definitely not help you."

"I'm *not* being defensive!" Sadie snipped. Coco stiffened in her arms and craned her tiny neck to stare at the detective as if backing Sadie up. She'd always been a loyal dog.

"*Really* not helpful," Broussard said in a similar tone. Under other circumstances, Sadie might have found his mimicked quip amusing. As it stood, she simply felt insulted.

"Broussard," one of the policemen called out. "Better come check this out."

"Sit down," Broussard told Sadie, indicating a chair as he walked over to see what the policeman had found. "And don't even think about going anywhere."

"Why would I?" Sadie said, exasperated. "I haven't done anything!"

Sadie took a seat, as directed, thankful that the Louis XV armchair added a bit of dignity to the humiliating situation.

"Don't worry, Coco," she said, patting the Yorkie's petite head. "They'll be back any minute to eat crow." Glancing at Coco, she added, "Don't get any ideas. It's just an expression."

Sadie waited patiently for the detective to return, certain an apology would be forthcoming. Instead, he returned with a stern look on his face, accompanied by the policemen. One held a small paper cup left over from Sadie's room service order the night before.

"Well, look what we have here," Broussard said, eying Sadie with suspicion.

"Hot chocolate?" Sadie said. "You needed a warrant to find hot chocolate? You could have ordered that from that other bakery, Bluette's.

"It's not hot chocolate," Broussard said. He opened the lid slowly with plastic-gloved hands. Tilting it forward, he showed the container to Sadie.

"Whipped cream?" Sadie said, confused. "I don't understand. What's the problem?"

"The problem," Broussard said, "is the toxicology report that we got back on the tart the victim ate. It tested positive for cyanide."

"In the tart?" Sadie said, both shocked at the revelation and relieved once again that she didn't order a tart to go on that fateful morning.

Broussard shook his head. "No, not in the tart itself. That was clear. But the whipped cream was heavily laced with cyanide."

Sadie's eyes widened. "Mimi Arnaud was *poisoned*? How dreadful! But that has nothing to do with me. Look, I'll show you." Quickly she set Coco down, jumped out of the chair, and plunged her finger into the whipped cream. She'd almost brought it to her mouth before Broussard grabbed her arm.

"No!" he shouted. He escorted Sadie to the suite's bathroom, keeping a firm grip on her arm. After scrubbing her finger with soap and water, he peeled off his plastic gloves. Returning to the front room, he asked the other men to bag the whipped cream container and dispose of his plastic gloves safely.

"I think a discussion at the station is in order," Broussard said.

"You're not arresting us?" Sadie asked, scooping Coco into her arms.

Both the policemen looked around as if another person were present.

"No, I'm not arresting you," Broussard said. "And we're certainly not in the habit of arresting dogs."

Sadie thought she saw a hint of a smile accompany the latter statement.

"You can ride with the officers here," Broussard said. "I'll meet you at the station."

"Fine," Sadie said. "Seeing as I'm not under arrest, I'll voluntarily offer to cooperate." Just the sound of her words made Sadie feel back in control. She was offering to help now, not merely going along with the detective's directions.

Sadie gathered up Coco, her tote bag, and her phone and accompanied the men to the police car. As she slid into the vehicle, a buzz from her cell phone indicated an incoming text. Once seated, she pulled out her phone to check it.

Meet at Bluette's at 9:30?

Sadie sighed. Beignets and café au lait with Clotile certainly sounded better than her current itinerary.

"You officers wouldn't care to stop at Bluette's Beignets on the way to the station, would you?" Sadie quipped as she waved her phone in the air. "They probably have donuts."

"Old joke," one of the officers said. "Not really funny."

"Well, I thought it was funny," she whispered to Coco as she sent a text back to Clotile.

Not this morning. A little indisposed at the moment.

Maybe indisposed was a bit of an understatement, but it avoided the more complicated, complete explanation. She waited for a return text and was relieved to see a simple response.

Okay. Maybe later.

Sadie typed a quick text. *Sounds good.*

TWELVE

The local police station was a stately building, solid and plain, lacking the enchanting ambiance of the balconies and architecture of the French Quarter. Yet it took only a short drive to get there, and Sadie soon found herself seated at a table in a sparsely furnished room.

"Detective Broussard will be with you in just a bit." The officer who hadn't appreciated her donut joke set a mug of coffee in front of Sadie, excused himself, and left the room.

On her own with nothing to do at the moment but wait for the detective, Sadie took Coco out of the tote bag, set the Yorkie on the table, and looked around. Contrary to movie scenes she's seen, no overhead light hung low over the table, the kind where someone's half-lit face might ask "Where were you the night of…" Instead, sunshine flowed through side windows, making the room feel more like a conference room in a business office than an interrogation room. It was basic but not unfriendly.

"What do you think, Coco?" Sadie said as she surveyed the area. "Nothing a few plants and framed artwork couldn't spruce up. Or maybe wallpaper… yes, something whimsical like jail cells with lavish décor and inmates toasting each other with champagne. Something like that. Wouldn't you agree?"

Getting a yip for a response, Sadie took it as a vote of approval. She slipped her hand into a side pocket and pulled out a small bone-shaped cookie, which Coco gladly accepted.

The petite canine was in the process of chomping on the treat when Detective Broussard entered the room. He held a coffee mug in one hand and a pen and paper in the other.

"Do you think... oh, never mind." The detective took a seat across from Sadie while casting skeptical looks in Coco's direction.

"So, Detective Broussard," Sadie said. "Why am I here if I'm not under arrest? And why did you come to search my room anyway? I don't understand any of this."

"Which do you want to know first? You're asking several questions at once." Broussard said. "Never mind, I'll just explain straight off. You're here because we think you can help us."

"Okay," Sadie said, unsure if she was going to like where this was going. She'd seen enough television shows where people were forced to wear wires and enter dangerous situations. She had Coco's safety to think about as well. With that thought, she picked Coco up off the table and held her close.

"And we came to your room because we received an anonymous tip that something you had would implicate you. The reason you're not under arrest is your reaction to the whipped cream," Broussard added. "If you'd known it was poisoned, you wouldn't have tried to eat it."

"What makes you even think it's poisoned?" Sadie said. "I just added that whipped cream to the hot chocolate I had late last night, and I'm fine."

"Did it smell like almonds last night?" Broussard asked.

"No," Sadie said. "Why would it?"

"If it had been the same whipped cream you had last night, it would have," Broussard said. "Well, that's not necessarily true," he said, qualifying his statement. "Cyanide has a strong almond smell, though not everyone's sense of smell recognizes it."

"So maybe I'm in the percentage of people who don't pick up on the almond smell," Sadie said. "That doesn't explain why I had it last night and yet am perfectly fine today. What's your explanation for that?"

"Easy," Broussard said. "It's not the same whipped cream. Someone had to have switched it out since last night."

"Are you saying someone went into my room?" Sadie leaned forward. "When?"

"Obviously between the time you had your hot chocolate and the time we searched your room this morning. Have you left your room since last night?"

Sadie shook her head. "Only to take Coco for a quick walk this morning."

"Any chance you left your room unlocked?"

"No," Sadie said, her voice firm. "I'm very careful about that when I travel." Sadie reached into a pocket, pulled out her room key, and placed it on the table. "I never leave this anywhere. I always know exactly where it is."

Coco reached out with one paw and swatted the key, sending it flying across the table and into Broussard's coffee mug with a sharp clink.

"Have you loaned it to anyone while you've been staying here?" The detective eyed Coco as he gently handed the key back to Sadie.

"Absolutely not," Sadie said.

Broussard tapped his fingers on the table. "I checked the lock and doorframe of your room when I left. It hasn't been tampered with."

"Meaning what? That someone else has a key to my room?" Sadie shuddered, suddenly glad she always secured the dead bolt and chain locks on hotel doors at night.

"That's the logical assumption," Broussard said. "Many

people at a hotel have access to a master key—housekeeping, maintenance, the front office..."

"Well!" Sadie huffed. "That's certainly not very comforting."

"Not in this case," Broussard agreed. "But if you had an emergency and they were able to get inside to help you, I imagine it would be."

Sadie had to admit the detective had a point. "I suppose so. But... do you think we're safe now?" She glanced at Coco and then back at Broussard. "Should we find another place to stay? I don't really want to change hotels if I don't have to." *And I might be able to find something out if I stay*, she thought to herself.

"I think you'll be safe staying. And you may be able to help us," Broussard said as if echoing her thoughts. "I can put a twenty-four-hour watch on your room."

"Won't that make the hotel suspicious?" Sadie asked. "If someone working there is the person who entered my room..." She shuddered again at the thought of someone in her room. In particular, the creepy face of Horace LeBlanc came to mind.

"We can watch without the hotel knowing," Broussard said as he jotted down notes to himself. "And I don't think you were the target of the whipped cream we found in your room. We believe it was put there to frame you, just to cast suspicion away from the real killer."

"Why me?" Sadie asked, not sure if she should feel insulted or honored.

Broussard looked up from the notepad. "Why *not* you? You were there at the bakery that morning, you're staying at the hotel that's linked to the family dispute, you just arrived in town, and you're planning to leave soon. You're a perfect target for framing."

Sadie sighed. Somehow that didn't make her feel especially

secure about traveling in the future, and she did love to travel. Even Coco had her own travel wardrobe.

"Keep your dead bolt and chain locked whenever you're in your room," Broussard said, standing up. We'll have eyes on your room when you go out, so we'll know if anyone tries to go in." He walked to the door, opened it, and called to the two officers, instructing them to take Sadie back to the hotel.

"Thank you for your cooperation, Ms. Kramer." Broussard shook her hand.

"Well, thank you for not arresting me," Sadie countered. "Coco thanks you too."

"You're welcome," Broussard said, adding after a brief hesitation, "both of you."

THIRTEEN

"That's just crazy," Clotile said. She took a sip from a tall, curved glass and looked at Sadie, shaking her head.

"Tell me about it," Sadie said. "This is not what I had in mind for a vacation." Sadie tasted her own drink, and her eyes lit up. "This, however, is fabulous. What did you order for us? I may need to have another after this." She looked around, taking in the happy-hour atmosphere at Cyril's Crazy Cajun Cookery. Jazz music flowed from overhead speakers, and an enthusiastic crowd surrounded a table of complimentary appetizers.

Clotile held her glass up in the air. "I bet you won't find these on those boardwalks at Fisherman's Wharf. We call this a Hurricane."

Sadie nodded approval. "Sweet and colorful. And I love the fruit and little umbrella on top. I feel like I'm on an exotic island."

"I'd say you are." Clotile laughed. "New Orleans isn't your everyday city. And you're having a wild week, that's for sure."

"Don't remind me," Sadie said. "I'd like to forget about everything for an hour or two."

"Well, a couple of Hurricanes might just do the trick," Clotile said.

Forgetting about all the drama had been her intention when she had decided to head over to the restaurant to meet up with

Clotile. She'd changed into black slacks and a rhinestone-studded fuchsia T-shirt and wrapped a multicolored scarf around her head. Skeleton-head earrings that she'd picked up on a quick excursion to the French Market that afternoon added an edgy touch to the outfit. At least Coco had thought so when she put them on. The Yorkie had backed away from the odd accessories at first but relaxed once Sadie let her bat them back and forth.

"In that case, I'm going to check out the appetizer table." Sadie stood up and hoisted her tote bag over her shoulder. "Any requests?"

"Popcorn shrimp, if they have it," Clotile said.

Sadie sauntered over to the crowded food area, certain she was blending in with the other happy-hour aficionados. Surveying the crowd, she wondered if she might even be taken for a local. She definitely fit in better than she had originally in her coastal seashell attire.

Searching the appetizer selections, she piled some chips on a small paper plate. She debated between several dips, finally choosing a hot crawfish concoction. Not seeing any resembling popcorn shrimp, she topped the plate off with some sort of fritters.

Ready to head back to the table, she took a few steps in that direction but suddenly stopped cold. A man stood next to Clotile, bent forward close enough to whisper in Clotile's ear. With his head lowered, Sadie couldn't make out his face, but he seemed familiar. At least he seemed familiar with Clotile, especially when he glanced around furtively and then placed a quick kiss on her cheek before patting her on the shoulder and walking away.

Sadie turned back toward the food in order to give herself time to think. Why didn't the man simply sit down at the table and join them? Had Clotile not invited him to? Perhaps she had, and he had other plans, so he declined. Or maybe it was something more. And was he leaning that close to her ear in order to be heard over the music? Or was it to not be heard by anyone else?

Taking a bite of a fritter, she closed her eyes, savoring the mixed flavors of shrimp, onion, and garlic. She debated the kiss she'd observed. Was it that of a friend? A cousin? A brother? Someone closer? She'd only known Clotile for a few days, not long enough to know much about her personal life. The man could have been anyone, perhaps someone she didn't even know. But why had he seemed familiar?

Sadie closed her eyes and tried to visualize the scene again. What had he been wearing? All she remembered was that it had been nondescript. What was his posture like? That was difficult to tell, seeing as he was bent over. Was he wearing a watch? Yes, something on his wrist had caught the light when he patted Clotile on her shoulder. Maybe...

"Are you all right?"

Sadie jumped at the recognizable voice. She opened her eyes to find Clotile standing in front of her, eyeing her with curiosity and concern.

"Of course I'm all right," Sadie said, perhaps too quickly. "Why?"

"Because you were standing here with your eyes closed, holding a fritter in front of your mouth, as if giving thanks to the inventor of fried foods, that's why." Clotile put her hands on her hips and tilted her head to the side. Even with her nerves on edge, Sadie fought back a smile. Clotile's description was undoubtedly accurate. That's exactly what she must have looked like.

"I was just savoring the flavor of this fritter," Sadie said hastily. "Delicious! I can't get over the fantastic use of spices in the food here."

"Cajun food is known for its flavor," Clotile said. "And it looks like you've got a good selection. I'll make myself a plate and meet you back at the table. I already ordered us a couple more drinks."

Sadie hesitated. "I'm not sure I need a second drink after all," she said. The thought occurred to her that lingering at the restaurant might not be the best decision at this point. On the other hand, she wasn't about to let the food on her plate go to waste.

"Then just drink half of it," Clotile said as she picked up a miniature crab cake and set it on her plate.

"Good suggestion," Sadie said, mostly as an excuse to get out of the conversation and move away. "I'll meet you back at the table."

Sadie returned to her seat and set the food down. She broke off part of a chip and dropped it into the tote bag and was rewarded with a yip of thanks.

"Great food selection," Clotile said as she sat back down, her plate loaded.

Now on her third shrimp fritter, Sadie couldn't disagree. She nodded her head in agreement and waited to speak until she'd swallowed. "Amazing they can put that spread out there for free. They could make do with just the chips and dips."

"It only seems free, trust me," Clotile said. "They make plenty on the extra drinks they sell because of the food. Liquor is always where the biggest profit is for restaurants."

"Yes, I've heard that before," Sadie said. "And they do seem to bring in a big crowd."

"They sure do," Clotile said. "Great for people-watching."

Why the small talk? Sadie wondered. *To cover up something?*

"I can see that," Sadie said. "It's quite the meeting place too. I imagine you run into people you know here."

"Not really," Clotile said. "People come here in groups, after work. Or they come alone, looking for a singles scene." She glanced around as if to confirm the presence of single customers there.

"Ah, yes," Sadie said. "We have plenty of places like that in California. The after-work crowd gathers, looking to forget the stress of the workday before heading home."

"Exactly." Clotile took a healthy gulp of her Hurricane.

Seeing an opening, Sadie decided to dig for information. "Speaking of work, I believe I told you I run a fashion boutique in San Francisco."

Although she'd intended her statement to lead to a discussion of what Clotile did for a living, this reminded her that she ought to check in with Amber, back in the shop. She wasn't worried, as the reliable assistant would have contacted her if needed. But it was her habit to check in anyway when away on trips.

"Yes," Clotile said. "You mentioned that on the airplane. That must be fun, working with clothing and accessories. In fact, I bet you could pick some things up at the French Market that you could sell at your own shop."

"Not a bad idea," Sadie answered truthfully. She could see the skeleton earrings appealing to the trendier customers.

"I don't recall what type of work you said you do," Sadie ventured. "I'm sorry. My memory isn't what it used to be."

"Don't worry. We're all getting on in years." Clotile looked around the room again and then looked back at Sadie. "I do a little of this and that. Nothing as exciting as owning my own fashion boutique." She took another sip and stood up. "Be right back. Must hit the ladies' room."

Great evasion tactic, Sadie thought as she watched Clotile walk away. *And not a bad time to prepare for my own escape.* She nibbled on her food, contemplating a departure plan.

"Much better," Clotile said as she returned to the table.

Must people always make comments after bathroom visits? It was a habit Sadie disliked. Then again, she didn't much like anything about the way the day had gone.

"I'd better be getting back to the hotel," Sadie said. She took one more sip of her Hurricane and dipped a chip into the crawfish dip, if only to not appear in a hurry to leave.

Clotile nodded. "Well, you have had quite a day."

"Indeed," Sadie said. "One I'd like to forget." She yawned and stood up. "Thank you for the... What did you call them? Oh yes, Hurricanes."

Sadie waved and headed out. As she started the walk back to the hotel, she confided in the only living creature she trusted at this point.

"Coco, I have a bad feeling about all this."

FOURTEEN

Sadie approached the hotel with caution, unsure if she felt rattled by the events at Cyril's Crazy Cajun Cookery or simply nervous about additional problems with her accommodations. Detective Broussard had promised the room would be watched at all times, but how did she know that for sure? Was the police watch that had been set up that dependable?

"We should have changed hotels, Coco," she said, head tilted toward her right shoulder, where her tote bag hung. "There's a lovely place just a block from here with wrought iron balconies and begonias along the railings. It's not our responsibility to help the police catch a killer, as convenient as it is for them to have us help." The tote bag swayed in response to her voice. "I understand, Coco," she responded. "I'm curious too. And getting more suspicious by the hour."

The courtyard outside her room was deserted, aside from a hotel maintenance worker repairing a sprinkler head. She said hello as she slid her room key into the lock. The man nodded a polite but disinterested greeting in return and went back to work.

Relieved to find the interior of the room untouched, Sadie helped Coco settle into her luxurious travel palace. She prepared the Yorkie's dinner, refilled her water bowl, and then retreated to the front room.

Grabbing a magazine from a side table, Sadie collapsed

on the couch, hoping a little mundane reading material would take her mind off the events of her supposed vacation. After reading one survey that turned her cheeks bright red, a shampoo ad with luxurious locks flowing off the page, and an article titled "Ten Days to Firm Abs!" Sadie tossed the magazine aside. She liked her shampoo, she'd grown to accept her soft muscles, and as for the survey? Well, those days were over.

A sudden ring from the suite's telephone caused Sadie to jump. Against her better judgment, she answered the call, relieved to find it was only a young girl at the front desk.

"Would you like any ice tonight, Ms. Kramer?"

Heavens, no! Sadie caught herself before spilling out the sentiment in those exact words. "No, thank you," she managed. "And it's fine to call me Sadie."

Hanging up the phone, Sadie glanced at her watch. It was early evening, yet she felt exhausted. The idea of dinner was unappealing. For one thing, she still felt stuffed from all the appetizers. For another, she'd survived the day and was now safely tucked back in her room. She wasn't about to go out again.

With that thought, she walked to the door and secured both the dead bolt and the chain. As far as she was concerned, she was in for the night. If she became hungry, she had her usual stash of snacks and chocolate on hand. If lonely, she had Coco to talk to—ideal since Coco had a wide range of expressive responses but didn't actually talk back. This made for a perfect conversation, especially when Sadie felt tired or confused, both of which she felt now.

Sadie glanced at the clock, noting that it was nearly eight p.m. Taking the time difference into consideration, she realized she could still reach Amber and see how things were going at Flair. Maybe the touch of familiarity that would come with checking in on her own business would calm her nerves. She picked up her cell phone and punched in the number to the boutique. Amber answered on the second ring.

"Sadie, I'm glad to hear from you!" Amber's voice was as perky as ever, likely due to the massive quantities of coffee she drank throughout the day.

"Why?" Sadie asked. "Is anything wrong?"

"Uh, no," Amber said. "Why would you think that? You know I'd call you if anything went wrong."

Sadie sighed. She could hear the clicking sound of hangers bumping against each other in the background, as well as muffled voices. That was a good sign; the shop was doing business. "I'm sorry, Amber. My nerves are on edge. I guess I just assume things are going to go wrong at this point."

"Aren't you on vacation, Sadie?" Amber asked. "You're not supposed to worry on vacation. You're supposed to get *away* from worrying. Why are your nerves on edge anyway? You're not in chocolate withdrawal, are you? They must have chocolate in New Orleans."

"Of course they do." Sadie laughed. She was glad to feel the mood lighten, although now she had visions of Matteo's mouthwatering chocolates in her head. Having a gourmet chocolatier next door to her San Francisco boutique had only made the chocolate cravings she'd had all her life grow stronger. "Am I missing out on any new flavor Matteo's created this week?"

"Just a passion fruit truffle with sprinkles of coconut on top," Amber said. "He said he'd recreate it for you when you return. He said your opinion is the most valuable."

"Such a sweet-talker," Sadie said. "But I don't object to

being his official taste-tester."

"I'm sure you don't." Amber laughed and then became more serious. "So tell me why your nerves are on edge. You didn't sound like yourself when this conversation started."

Sadie sighed. Where to begin? "Let's just say I stumbled into another mystery."

"That seems to happen when you travel," Amber pointed out.

"I know," Sadie admitted. "I guess I just have a knack of being in the wrong place at the wrong time."

"This isn't another…" Amber lowered her voice to a whisper, an additional sign that customers were present. "…murder, is it?"

"I'm afraid so," Sadie said. She proceeded to explain the series of events, pausing once when Amber excused herself to answer a customer's question.

"Well, at least you've made a friend there," Amber said when she was back on the line. "How fortunate to meet someone on the airplane who lives there and can show you around."

"That's what I thought until today," Sadie said, going on to explain the odd interaction at the restaurant earlier.

"I don't know," Amber said. "Please don't take this the wrong way, but I can hear how on edge you are. Could you be reading more into it than there is?"

"I might be," Sadie admitted. "But it bothers me that the man Clotile talked to seemed familiar. I keep trying to place him."

"Maybe he's the hotel owner you said arrived in town recently?"

"No, I don't think so," Sadie said. "Clotile didn't seem to know him when she pointed him out during the wine-and-appetizer hour. She knew who he was, but that was all. I got the impression she knew the man at the restaurant well."

"Because? Wait, just a minute." Amber set the phone down to ring up a sale. Sadie heard her thank the customer before coming back on the line.

"Because?" Amber repeated.

"It was the way she responded to the man's affection," Sadie said. "It was more than a casual happy-hour flirtation. And she didn't mention it afterward. I think she would have bragged a little about a stranger flirting with her."

"So you think she was hiding something," Amber said.

"Yes, or…" Sadie paused. "Wait. Something just occurred to me. There's another possibility. She might have been scared."

"Now you've lost me," Amber said. "How did flirtation turn into fear?"

"The way he patted her shoulder when he left. It was more than a gentle tap. In fact, it looked firm, as if underscoring whatever he whispered to her."

"Okay," Amber said, clearly still confused.

Sadie stood up and began pacing. "Yes, why didn't I see this before? I think she was scared. That explains why she was glancing around after we sat back down. It also explains why she didn't mention it."

"Are you going to talk to her about it?" Amber asked.

"I don't know," Sadie said. "What if I'm wrong about her being scared? What if she's involved with all this? Letting her know I saw the man approach her at the restaurant could put me in even more danger."

Sadie ended the call with Amber and put her phone away. Sinking back into the couch cushions, she realized her biggest problem of all: she no longer knew whom to trust.

FIFTEEN

S adie glanced up at the sign hanging over the entrance to the fortune-teller's shop. As silly as it seemed to the logical side of her brain, the other side wanted to hear what the fortune-teller had to say again. She'd certainly predicted events correctly during the first visit, saying someone was in danger. Granted, that was the type of general statement that could cover a lot of bases. Sadie knew it was just a line used for dramatic effect. Still, it *had* turned out to be true. She couldn't help but wonder what else the woman might foretell.

The interior of the shop looked just as it had the first night she'd wandered in. Voodoo items, potions, pamphlets, skulls, and souvenirs all lined multiple shelves, enticing tourists to pick up bizarre artifacts to take home to family and friends.

A young man worked behind the counter this time, multiple tattoos and piercings accentuating his youthful face and body. A stick of incense extended upward from a jar of sand, its scent blending in seamlessly with the rest of the shop's décor. Music that Sadie now recognized as zydeco blasted from speakers at a volume several levels higher than she would have thought ideal.

Sadie approached the counter and set her tote bag on its surface. Distracted momentarily by an ink design of a crow on the clerk's neck that oddly complemented the word Crow on his name tag, she refocused quickly and explained the purpose of her visit.

"We'd like to see the fortune-teller."

As often happened when she phrased comments in such a way, the young man glanced around to see who accompanied her. Whether out of good manners or simply confusion, he looked back at Sadie and said, "Sure." Picking up the shop phone, he arranged an appointment. Fifteen minutes later, Sadie and Coco sat in the back room, in front of a round table.

Gina entered through a side door that creaked as she closed it. She wore a flowing dress of gauzy mustard-colored material, cinched in at the waistline with multiple bands of scarves. Gold chains intertwined with the fabric, much in the way someone might braid hair. Long strands of beads dangled from her neck, resting at varying heights. Her hair was swept up in a loose topknot, feathers sticking out in different directions.

"You are here again," Gina said after settling into the seat across from Sadie. Her voice was solemn, as if the declaration told of things to come.

"Yes," Sadie said, attempting—with some difficulty—to match Gina's serious tone.

"I'm glad to see you," Gina said. She opened a black enamel box with mother of pearl inlay, removed a match, and lit a votive candle in the center of the table. Sadie watched a spiral of smoke evaporate into the air when the woman blew out the match.

"What brings you in today?" Gina placed both palms down on the table and leveled a gaze so direct that Sadie shifted uncomfortably in her seat.

Maybe this wasn't such a good idea after all, Sadie thought. She patted her tote bag gently, as if to calm her own nerves by calming Coco. This gesture was ridiculous, she realized, as she had no way of knowing if the woman's demeanor was troubling to Coco or not.

"Wait." Gina raised both hands in the air dramatically. "You don't need to tell me. I can see it in your eyes. You are troubled."

"Yes," Sadie said. "I'd say that pretty much sums it up."

Gina closed her eyes. She inhaled slowly, exhaled just as slowly, and opened her eyes again. "It is telling that you use the word 'sums,'" she said. "You have more than one trouble in your life right now."

I've actually lost count at this point, Sadie said to herself.

"Yes," Sadie replied out loud.

"This trip has not been what you expected," Gina said.

"No," Sadie said but then rephrased. "I should say both yes and no."

"Ah," Gina said knowingly, but she didn't continue. Instead, she leaned forward, the light from the candle reflecting unevenly across her features. "Tell me about your time here in New Orleans. What is 'yes' and what is 'no'?"

Coco picked that exact moment let out a sharp yip, causing both Sadie and Gina to look at the tote bag, which Sadie had cradled in her lap. Coco's head popped up above the edge of the bag. A tiny rhinestone barrette that Sadie had clipped into Coco's head earlier shimmered in the candlelight. Sadie pulled a treat out of the tote's outside pocket and held it out to Coco, who eagerly took it and disappeared back into the bag.

"The 'yes,'" Sadie said, turning her attention back to Gina, "includes the jambalaya and gumbo, the colors and curiosities of the French Market, the architecture of the historic buildings, and the fascinating music."

An odd buzz interrupted the session. Glancing at the side of the table, Sadie was surprised to see an incoming call on a cell phone.

"I'm so sorry. I didn't realize I'd left that out," Gina said. She picked up the phone, turned it off, and slipped it under the table.

Just another case of someone's personal life interfering with the day job. "Don't even worry about it," Sadie said.

"And the 'no'?" Gina asked, continuing on as if the cell phone hadn't disrupted the session at all.

Where do I even begin? Sadie thought to herself. *Or, better yet, don't begin at all.*

This internal warning took her by surprise. On the edge of summarizing the negative aspects of her visit, she realized a simple truth: Gina could be a local, just like anyone else with a day job. She might know someone who knew someone who knew someone involved with the whole crazy Arnaud-LeBlanc mess.

On the other hand, the fortune-teller might simply be an accountant from Baton Rouge who commuted into New Orleans for a part-time job as a distraction from her regular work. Certainly dressing up as she did would be a change of pace.

"Now that I think about it," Sadie said lightly, "there really isn't a 'no.'" This city is rich with culture, and the people are fascinating. I'd say the trip has turned out to be even more interesting than I expected it to be." *There*, Sadie thought, feeling clever. *An understatement is a way to tell the truth without telling the whole truth.*

"I see," Gina said, nodding knowingly. "Let's see what the cards have to say." She moved the candle to the side of the table and brought out a deck of tarot cards. One by one, she arranged the cards face up.

Sadie watched each card as it emerged from the deck, intrigued by the vintage designs: a fool, dancing on the edge of a cliff; a magician, arm held high above a chalice; a dog and wolf howling at a moon; an emperor, dressed in armor, on a throne.

"You are looking for a solution to your problems," Gina said. Bangles on her arm jangled as she reached out and tapped the magician card. "But beware of illusion."

"Illusion," Sadie repeated slowly, as if hearing the word for the first time.

"Yes," Gina said. "Things are not always as they seem."

Sadie nodded. "I'm finding that out."

Gina moved her hand to another card. "Do you see what the emperor is wearing?"

Sadie leaned forward, studying the image. "A robe."

"True," Gina said. "But what else?"

Again Sadie looked at the man's attire. "He's also wearing armor."

"Exactly," Gina said. "You are up against real power." Her hand moved back to the magician card. "Yet there is a possibility of illusion."

"That's not a comfortable combination," Sadie said, feeling rattled in spite of her skepticism about tarot cards in general. The fortune-teller did seem to be hitting on points that related to her current predicament, whether by accident or not.

The tote bag shifted in her lap, a sign that Coco was getting restless. This was a sign Sadie could interpret herself. *There will be a walk in the near future.*

"I'm sorry to cut the session short, Gina, but I must go now," Sadie said, standing up. "To be more specific, the creature in my tote bag must go now."

"I understand." Gina maintained her fortune-teller voice, yet grinned. "I have a similar creature at home."

Sadie thanked Gina and left the shop. Conveniently, a

grassy area was a short walk away. As she took Coco on the much-needed walk, Gina's words echoed in her mind.

You are up against great power, but watch out for illusion.

SIXTEEN

Bluette's Beignets was just as crowded as Sadie expected it to be. With Lisette's place still closed across the street, most tables were filled with cheerful diners. Other customers stood to the side, numbered tickets in hand, waiting for orders to take back to offices.

Fortunately, a few tables remained unoccupied. Sadie headed for a two-top in a side area. It was a perfect location for not being disturbed. She sat in one chair, back to the wall, and gave Coco the other—which is to say she set her bag on that chair, claiming both seats. She had no interest in anyone joining her. All she wanted to do was think and observe. Her simple outfit—jeans, a purple shirt, and a wide-brimmed hat she'd picked up at a boutique near Marie Laveau's—would help her blend in as well. She'd even resisted adding the earrings with glittery clusters of grapes that she usually loved to wear with that particular blouse.

Business was booming. Bluette—Sadie recognized her immediately from the description Clotile had given here—stood behind the cash register, quietly ringing up sales. In addition, a server moved from table to table, taking and delivering orders in an attempt to keep the line from building up at the counter.

A pony-tailed girl who barely looked old enough to drive approached Sadie's table. She wore a name tag that said Marie.

"Welcome to Bluette's Beignets. What may I get you?"

Marie sported the determined look of someone proud of her first foray into the workforce. She posed a pen against an order pad as if expecting a complicated order. Sadie had no doubt this was the girl's first job, if not her first day. There was something both sweet and impressive in the way the server took her role so seriously.

"What do you recommend?" Sadie asked.

"The beignets are a favorite," Marie replied. She then leaned forward as if divulging a personal secret. "But I love the apple fritters myself."

Sadie contemplated, arriving at the most reasonable answer. "Then I'd better try both! I'll take one of each. And a small bag to take the two halves I'll be saving for later."

"Café au lait with that? Or something else?"

"Hot tea," Sadie said. "With a slice of lemon, if that's possible."

"Of course." The girl jotted the order down on the notepad. "Coming right up."

Sadie sat back and looked around the room, thinking about Gina's words. The whole fortune-telling scenario seemed more show than anything, but the woman's comments about illusion had hit home. Sadie already felt she couldn't trust anyone she'd met on the trip. Wasn't that a question of illusion? How could one know if people were what they seemed or if they only appeared to be? This was especially true when traveling and meeting strangers, without adequate time for more than a casual acquaintance.

Normally these types of thoughts wouldn't bother Sadie. She had a small circle of friends at home and trusted them completely. Amber ran her boutique, Flair, with the same care she would if it were her own shop. Matteo, aside from keeping her chocolate cravings satisfied, was always there for her when she needed someone to talk to. And, of course, there was Coco, loyal, true blue. There was no question of illusion in her circle of friends.

"Here you go: one beignet, one apple fritter, one pot of tea with lemon, and a bag for whatever you take to go. Enjoy." The server slid the plates onto the table and moved on.

One bite of beignet had Sadie practically melting with satisfaction. The powdered sugar was the perfect companion to the delicious fried dough of the donut-type pastry itself. She squeezed the lemon into the tea, took a sip, and followed it by tasting the apple fritter that the young server had recommended. Delicious!

Her train of thought was interrupted by the sound of a man coughing at a nearby table. He faced the opposite direction, his back to her. A sudden fear gripped her, wondering if she was about to see a repeat of the scene with Mimi Arnaud. If so, she would swear off bakeries forever. After all, she could always make the sacrifice of living on chocolate alone. Matteo would take care of her.

Her fear subsided when she realized the customer was not choking but simply coughing to get the attention of a customer who had just entered, another man.

"What do you think, Coco?" Sadie said as she dropped a crumb of beignet into her tote bag. "Couldn't he just have called out the man's name? Or summoned him over by waving his arm? People are so funny sometimes." Coco yipped, and Sadie dropped another crumb. "I'm surprised the man even heard him over this noisy crowd."

Taking another sip of tea, Sadie found herself surprisingly irked by the man's cough, thinking at first it was just because it seemed an odd way to get someone's attention. But it didn't take long for her to realize the real reason the gesture seemed odd: it was the particular cough itself. It was familiar, recognizable. It matched the cough she'd heard in the alley the first night.

Sadie pulled her hat's brim lower over her forehead and held the apple fritter in front of her face, as if about to take a bite. She realized she must look like she was holding one of the masks she'd admired at the French Market, though certainly tastier. But it was a means to an end, and it worked. There was no illusion in what she now saw. As she watched the two men meet, she had a clear glimpse of their faces as they shook hands before sitting back down. The man summoned by the cough was Horace LeBlanc. And the cough itself belonged to the man she'd seen with Clotile. In addition, he looked like the man she'd seen at the food counter at the French Market.

"If only we'd chosen a closer table," Sadie whispered to Coco. "We could have heard their conversation." Even as she said this, she realized it wouldn't have helped. The men had their heads lowered over paperwork. Their voices wouldn't have been loud enough to hear.

Sadie watched as the young server approached the table. Horace LeBlanc efficiently shooed the girl away as the other man turned the papers face down discreetly but quickly. After the server moved away, Horace walked to the counter and ordered on his own, bringing two mugs of coffee back to the table.

"Very secretive, don't you think, Coco?" Sadie leaned over her tote as if expecting an answer. "And who *is* this other man anyway?"

The flurry of bakery activity rose and fell as locals stopped by for their favorites and tourists popped in to try sweet New Orleans delicacies. Tables filled and emptied, yet the two men continued their hushed conversation.

"There's nothing to be gained in watching these men from afar," Sadie said to Coco finally. "It's obvious they're up to something, but I can't hear anything they're saying, and I can't see the paperwork." *Oh, how I'd love to see those papers!*

Gathering the tote into her lap, Sadie pulled out a tip for the server and tucked it alongside the pot of tea. She slid the partial portions of the beignet and apple fritter servings—not quite half of each, she admitted to herself—and was beginning to stand, when she saw Clotile walk in the front door.

Quickly Sadie dropped back into her seat and pulled the brim of her new hat down, relieved that Clotile couldn't recognize it. Tucking her tote bag under the table, out of sight, she watched Clotile walk directly over to the men and stand with her back to Sadie. This stance was convenient in the sense that Sadie was out of Clotile's line of sight. But it was inconvenient, as well, since there was no way of knowing Clotile's disposition. It only took a few seconds, however, to determine the disposition of the men. Both their faces were stern, almost icy. It was as if a mask of socially acceptable disapproval covered up an intense rage that had no place in public display.

As opposed to when the server had passed by, neither man had bothered to turn the papers face down, even when Clotile tapped her index finger pointedly on them.

"Clotile already knows whatever they're involved with, Coco," Sadie whispered. *Which means she's involved too. I knew it!*

Except that didn't entirely make sense. Why would all three be upset, in that case? There was only one logical explanation: whatever plan the three of them had started off with had now turned into a plan for two. And Clotile was no longer part of the "in" crowd.

As if to confirm Sadie's suspicions, Clotile abruptly turned and walked out, leaving the two men exchanging smug glances in her wake. Soon after, both men left, the paperwork safely tucked away inside Horace's jacket. That is, all but one sheet, which floated to the ground as they walked out the door.

"Well!" Sadie whispered to Coco. "We just can't have people littering, can we? No, I didn't think so!" Sadie made a quick departure, pausing just long enough at the doorway to pick the paper up and stash it in her bag.

SEVENTEEN

S adie entered the courtyard of the hotel, holding her tote bag securely against her side as if guarding precious gems. After all, Coco was more valuable than any gemstones could be. But she also suspected the paper she'd picked up had value in itself.

A middle-aged woman who was busy pruning rosebushes nodded hello. She wore overalls, a white T-shirt, and a denim hat with the embroidered wording, Cajun Clippers. To the side of the slogan, a cartoonish crawfish held a pair of pruning shears.

"Some surveillance, Coco," Sadie said after they entered the room and locked the door. "Though I must say, I wouldn't want to pick a fight with those pruning shears."

Coco—not having had more than a few crumbs at Bluette's Beignets—moved into eager position alongside her china food dish. While Sadie could hardly wait to inspect the paper that Horace had dropped, she understood that Coco's priorities at the moment differed from hers.

"Chicken, turkey, or salmon?" Sadie said, holding up cans of the Yorkie's favorite dinner fare. She watched as Coco surveyed the options, remaining indecisive. "Okay, salmon it is then." She emptied a can into a china bowl and added a few bites of kibble, just for the crunch of it. "There you go, Coco. That should keep you busy while I do a little reading."

Eagerly, Sadie pulled the paper from her bag but was

interrupted by an incoming text before she could look at it. Glancing at her phone's screen, she drew in a quick breath.

We need to talk!

Clotile. And the "tone" of the text sounded nothing like that of the Clotile she'd known for the past few days. Obviously, the scene she'd witnessed at Bluette's had changed Clotile's attitude in some way. Unsure how to respond, she set the phone aside and looked at the paper.

"What do you make of this, Coco?" Sadie asked. Not expecting a response, she continued on her own. "It's some sort of map."

Sadie moved to a nightstand, where the light was brighter, and looked at the paper closely. "No, it actually shows a couple of maps. Wait, there's some fine print here… Oh, fiddlesticks, Coco! Where are my reading glasses?" This brought a return look of surprise from Coco. If a Yorkie could be capable of raising eyebrows, it would describe the look she received.

Fetching her favorite reading glasses—black-and-white zebra print with rhinestones in the upper outside corners— she sat down on the edge of the bed to further investigate the contents of the paper Horace had unknowingly left behind for her.

Sadie, you there? I really need to talk to you.

Sadie sighed. Another text from Clotile. How was Sadie supposed to reply? She'd already determined that she couldn't trust anyone, perhaps least of all Clotile. The woman had seemed like such a pleasant acquaintance on the plane flight. But it seemed every place she'd led Sadie played some part in a bigger picture.

Chez Lisette's Patisserie, for example, where she walked right into a murder scene. And it was at the hotel's wine-and-appetizer hour that Horace had first appeared and Clotile had pointed him out. Then there was the episode at Cyril's Crazy Cajun Cookery, with the strange kiss and overly firm pat on the shoulder by the other man, the one now obviously connected with Horace.

Who is that man anyway? Sadie wondered.

To top it all off, the interaction she'd observed at Bluette's Beignets today cinched her suspicions. These people, including Clotile, were involved in something together.

Another thought suddenly hit her. Would she be in danger if she answered the text from Clotile? Or would she be in *more* danger if she didn't?

Sadie decided to buy herself some time to think.

Here. BRB.

That should do it, she thought. She'd acknowledged the text so Clotile wouldn't think she was ignoring her. Yet "BRB" AKA "be right back" would work as a stalling tactic.

Going back to the paper, Sadie slipped on her zebra reading glasses and examined the maps. Now that she was able to read the small print, she was disappointed to find it didn't offer much information. Phrases like "Preliminary sketches," "first," "second," and "draft" did little to enlighten her. The initials "LMNOP" were scribbled at the bottom, but it didn't sound familiar. In fact, it sounded ridiculous. Was the person who drew the sketches also practicing the alphabet?

Taking a closer look, Sadie could see there was no address or contact name, though there was a phone number. She contemplated calling but decided against it. She seemed to be in enough trouble as it was. If this was part of something shady, as it certainly appeared to be, she didn't need these people to have her cell phone number. And calling from the hotel phone was out of the question.

How Sadie wished Horace LeBlanc had dropped all the

papers instead of just one. Then again, he probably would have realized he'd done that, leaving her with nothing. At least she had a tidbit of information.

Or was it only a tidbit?

Sadie took a closer look at the sketches. There was something familiar about them, at least about one portion. The shape of a subsection looked familiar, with two small opposing diagonal lines indicating… doors? That would make it a room. And the shape…

It's the hotel lobby! This realization puzzled Sadie. If that was the lobby, the rest of that sketch must indicate other rooms. Yes, there were other doors sketched in, yet they didn't match the hallways the way she remembered them.

Suddenly Sadie let out a loud laugh. Coco scurried onto the velvet pillow in her travel palace, as if her human had lost her mind.

"Coco!" Sadie said, still chuckling. "This whole thing is nonsense. They're simply discussing a remodel of the hotel."

Shaking her head, Sadie reached for her phone to text Clotile back, but then she paused. Something still wasn't right. Clotile had been much too upset to have it simply be over a hotel remodel. And what did she have to do with the hotel anyway?

As if that weren't enough to cast doubt on the overlapping situations, Mimi Arnaud was still dead, Sadie had still been set up for the murder with the switch of the whipped cream in her room's fridge, and Clotile, Horace, and Mystery Man were in the midst of a disagreement that seemed like more than a difference of opinion over remodeling plans.

No, there were too many overlapping occurrences and too many unanswered questions. And she had a feeling Clotile was her best link to the answers. But how could she approach

Clotile safely, not knowing what her particular involvement was?

A public place, Sadie thought. We can meet in a place that's at least somewhat safe since we'll be surrounded by other people. Would Bluette's be safe enough?

It was worth a try. And maybe Detective Broussard was fond of the beignets there. Yes, that would be the best bet. She'd invite both Clotile and the detective to breakfast, only Broussard could sit somewhere unobserved.

Sadie typed in a quick text.

Exhausted tonight. How about Bluette's at nine thirty tomorrow morning?

She waited nervously for the return text, hoping Clotile wouldn't push for a meeting that evening. Fortunately, she was in luck.

Fine. Nine thirty at Bluette's. See you then.

EIGHTEEN

S adie had to admit Detective Broussard looked impressive in bike shorts, a tank top, and running shoes. If she were twenty years younger, she might have been tempted to flirt with him. She might have even worn something youthful and hip, rather than the semi frumpy attire she'd chosen for the occasion. A shorter skirt and off-the-shoulder blouse maybe. Instead, her orange capris and oversized yellow tunic would have to do. At least she'd remembered to pack her plastic banana earrings and matching watchband for accessories.

"He must be a morning person, Coco," she said aloud, earning an odd look from a customer at the table next to hers.

Odd looks from strangers were something Sadie was used to. She didn't always think to whisper when speaking to the Yorkie in public. Most people didn't hold conversations with inanimate objects, in this case, a tote bag, by all appearances. Then again, the recent habit people had of wearing earbud microphones for phone calls did add some normalcy to the habit. At least she had a physical object as the recipient of her comments, rather than appearing to converse with nothing but air.

The detective had taken a table in the center of Bluette's Beignets. Facing the door, he could see customers who entered, yet the brim of his baseball cap, combined with the newspaper he held in front of his coffee, helped him blend in with the rest of the crowd.

Marie, the same young server who'd waited on her the last visit, approached Sadie's table and offered her coffee. She accepted readily, in spite of having downed two cups in the hotel lobby earlier. Caffeine didn't affect her nerves as much as it did some people. And she could use all the help she could get to stay on top of the anticipated discussion ahead of her.

"Would you like anything from our bakery selections to go with that?" Marie asked.

"Absolutely!" Sadie said. "I read about calas fried rice fritters when I was planning my visit here. I'm not sure what they are exactly, but it sounded like something I should try."

Marie smiled. "You'll love them. They have just a touch of cinnamon and vanilla."

"Count me in then. A person can't go wrong with cinnamon and vanilla," Sadie said.

Marie jotted a note on her order pad and walked away.

Sadie sat back and took a sip of coffee. In spite of nervous anxiety over the expected meeting with Clotile, she wanted to enjoy one of the best aspects of coffee establishments: people-watching. Especially when traveling, a lot could be told through observation. Locals and tourists could usually be distinguished by both dress and mannerisms. And, if she couldn't figure out anything about a person, she could always make it up.

"Coco," she whispered, not wanting to draw the attention of nearby tables again, "you see that lady sitting in the corner with the blue streak in her hair? She's a figure-skating star but isn't expected to win the next competition because she's distraught over her ex-lover who ran off to Tahiti with her best friend." It sounded plausible enough, Sadie thought to herself with satisfaction. But she could do better.

"And that short guy at the counter? He's on parole for grand theft. I wonder if he'll pay for his order. I bet he stole those alligator boots he's wearing." She tapped her fingers on the table disapprovingly.

Sadie's face lit up as Marie set a plate of the rice fritters in front of her. The aroma of hot fried batter mixed with powdered sugar was intoxicating. She took a bite, closed her eyes, and sighed. What could be better than enjoying regional specialties? It was one of her priorities when traveling, much to the dismay of her waistline.

"Now, Coco," she continued to whisper. "I'm sure you saw that man in the jogging clothes at the middle table. He's a famous billionaire disguised as a marathon runner in order to keep from being recognized. He's madly in love with a fashion boutique owner from San Francisco but can't get the nerve up to tell her. He sends her anonymous gifts constantly—French perfume, emerald earrings, even a vintage brocade ceremonial kimono from Japan." She took another sip of coffee. "Of course she sends it all back. She does have principles, after all!"

Amused with herself, Sadie shook her head, banana earrings flopping back and forth. She took another bite of fried rice fritter, searched for another subject with an intriguing, albeit fictional, background.

"Here we go," Sadie whispered to Coco, who briefly stuck her head out of the tote bag to look around. "You see that lady walking in the door with the cane? She could use a style makeover—such drab clothing, not to mention the disheveled hair and odd hat."

Coco made a slight snorting sound and ducked back inside the tote bag.

"I know, not very nice of me to comment on her attire,"

Sadie admitted. "Not everyone has a "Flair" for style. But she can't help the limp. She was fortunate to survive the trapeze accident she had when she was performing in Europe. Now she works as an accountant, which is difficult since her eyes are so sensitive to light—thus the sunglasses she's wearing."

Sadie sighed with sympathy. "Some people's lives just don't go in a positive direction. And speaking of direction..." She paused as the woman looked around and then approached Sadie's table. Without invitation, she slid into the chair across from Sadie, took off her sunglasses, and set them down.

"Sadie," the now-recognizable woman said.

"Clotile," Sadie responded, unsure if she'd categorize her reaction as surprised, startled, or nervous. She rubbed her forehead as a means of surreptitiously shooting a sideways glance at Detective Broussard. Reassured that he'd noticed Clotile's arrival, she looked back at the well-disguised woman.

"Well, at least you didn't suffer a trapeze accident."

Clotile stared at her blankly.

"Never mind," Sadie said, waving her hand in the air. "The explanation wouldn't make any sense."

"I imagine you have some questions." Clotile ventured a tentative smile.

"More than you can possibly imagine," Sadie said. "Where should I begin? Oh, let's start with why you tried to poison me."

"Why I *what*?" Clotile raised her voice and then lowered it again quickly.

The conversation paused abruptly as Marie approached the table to see if the person who'd joined Sadie's table wanted to order anything. Clotile shook her head, and the server walked away.

"You know," Sadie continued. "The poison you planted in my room."

Clotile paled. "I have no idea what you're talking about!"

Sadie watched as the blood drained from Clotile's face. Unless the woman had the ability to turn into a ghost on cue, she was telling the truth.

"The whipped cream." Sadie tried for a different reaction.

"You mean at Lisette's?" Clotile said. "On Mimi's tart?"

"No, in my refrigerator," Sadie said. "Wait… what? You're the one who poisoned Mimi Arnaud at Lisette's?"

Even with Detective Broussard a few tables away, Sadie had the sudden impulse to run from the room.

Clotile leaned forward. "I did not poison Mimi Arnaud!" she whispered. "What on earth are you talking about?"

"I think you know," Sadie said. "Did they bribe you to do it?"

"Who are 'they'?" Clotile said, aghast. "And what do you mean by 'bribe' me? You think someone could bribe me to poison someone? Are you insane?"

"Well, it does appear you could use a clothing allowance," Sadie quipped as she looked Clotile up and down. "And a hairstylist," she added for good measure.

Clotile did not look amused.

"I'll have you know there is an undercover detective in this room," Sadie said. "So if you lured me here with bad intentions, I wouldn't suggest trying anything."

Clotile nodded. "I'm glad he's here. Or she, whatever."

"You're glad?" Sadie said. *Odd reply in view of the circumstances.* "Why?"

"This is why," Clotile said. She walked to the counter and returned quickly with a napkin and pen. She scribbled a short note and turned the napkin toward Sadie, who read it and then locked eyes with Clotile as the words sank in.

We're both in danger.

NINETEEN

The wine-and-appetizer hour in the hotel lobby looked especially scrumptious. Smoked paprika-glazed Andouille sausage, thin slices of Gouda, and crusty bread crisps were a perfect complement to the light-bodied French Burgundy the hotel was serving that evening.

Sadie took an appetizer selection, along with a glass of wine, to a seat purposely chosen to be within view of the front desk. Although she had no intention of glancing in that direction, Horace LeBlanc might happen to look out and see her. She figured her very public seating selection would send a signal that she was not aware of the situation Clotile had described. In other words, appearing to be oblivious to any danger might lower the danger she seemed to be in. It was a decent theory, in any case.

As skeptical as she'd been of Clotile's story, it seemed to be in her best interest to assume it was the truth. She had nothing else to go on unless Detective Broussard came up with something different. And so far he hadn't.

Thinking back to earlier in the day, she reviewed the conversation she'd had with the detective after meeting with Clotile. The plan they'd arranged beforehand, to leave separately and meet at another location, had been wise. Sadie had left Bluette's place shortly after Clotile—purposely not leaving with her—and spent ten minutes or so browsing shops along Bourbon Street. Intrigued by a glow-in-the-dark, faux-skull bracelet at one souvenir shop, she'd almost forgotten the plan to meet Broussard in front of Preservation Hall. From there they walked to Jackson Square, where they could mingle among others who gathered to enjoy artists who displayed their wares and musicians who entertained the crowds.

"You believe her," Broussard had said, phrasing it more as a statement than a question.

"Yes. She seems truly scared. She has no reason to make up such a wild story." Sadie had pointed that out while admiring a colorful painting of musical instruments dotting a night sky like stars. Although she'd resisted the temptation to buy it, the piece would have looked perfect in her own living room.

Broussard had insisted he bring Clotile into the station for questioning. Sadie had convinced him to let her talk Clotile into going in on her own, thinking she'd be more willing to cooperate if she felt the meeting was on her terms.

Sadie had considered telling the detective about the paper that Horace LeBlanc dropped. But discussing a hotel remodel paled in importance when compared to the more pressing issue of Clotile's involvement—or lack thereof—in Mimi Arnaud's death.

Now, over a sip of wine, Sadie pondered how exactly to convince Clotile to go in to talk to Detective Broussard. She'd made a point of not inviting Clotile to the hotel for appetizers, in order to give herself time to think. She still didn't know how completely she should trust Clotile's story. There were inconsistencies that bothered her. What about the other man she'd seen Horace LeBlanc with? Clotile refused to talk about him, even though Sadie had seen them together before. When Sadie pressed for information, Clotile hadn't denied knowing him but didn't want to talk about him. Other than saying he was working some kind of business deal with Horace, she'd pleaded ignorance of any details. Instead, she'd just encouraged Sadie to remove herself from danger by changing hotels or even returning to San Francisco earlier than planned.

Sadie wasn't about to leave New Orleans early. And she wasn't about to change hotels either. Not before she found out what was going on. Someone had tried to frame her, after all. She wasn't about to let that go. Besides, the appetizers were delicious. Why take the risk of having only pretzels or something similar at another lodging establishment? No, she'd chosen Hotel Arnaud-LeBlanc for a variety of reasons. The addition of mysterious goings-on was simply a bonus—aside from the detail of being in danger, of course.

Taking another trip to the appetizer table, Sadie could see the front desk out of the corner of her eye. Although she was not about to look directly, she could tell a tall figure stood behind the counter. *Undoubtedly, Horace LeBlanc*, she thought as she helped herself to another serving of Gouda, sausage, and crusty bread, as well as an extra slice of bread for Coco. "You'd love the sausage," she whispered to the Yorkie, "but the spices wouldn't be good for you."

Heading back to her room, she passed the same maintenance worker who'd been repairing the sprinkler head the other day. He now occupied a position a few rungs up on a ladder, replacing a rain gutter.

"Is it going to rain?" Sadie asked. She hoped not. The sunny weather so far had made it easy to explore the area. Besides, she hadn't brought her favorite raincoat with her. The bright yellow waterproof garment with rubber duckies on it always drew compliments or at least comments of some sort. Admittedly, some were better described as observations than compliments, and a few were borderline rude. It didn't bother

her in the least. She was very fond of that raincoat. Coco even had one to match.

"Not in the next few days, ma'am," the man said. "We just like to be prepared."

"Good," Sadie said, relieved. "Very good."

Inside the room, Sadie settled Coco in the travel palace and helped herself to a bottle of sparkling water. Opening the refrigerator to get the water gave her pause, but the police had assured her everything in her room was safe now.

Sitting on the edge of the bed, across from Coco, Sadie thought back to the unsettling whipped cream incident in her room. Whoever planted that was trying to throw the blame on her for Mimi Arnaud's death. Horace LeBlanc seemed the most likely suspect, seeing as he surely had a master key to the building. It would have been easy for him to slip in and out while she took Coco for the brief walk that morning. Would that mean he was the killer? It only stood to reason that the killer would be the one trying to divert attention to someone else.

Or maybe it *was* Clotile, and everything she was supposedly confiding now was simply an additional cover-up. Clotile's recent revelations at the café could all be lies. She might have intended to kill Mimi from the start.

Still, it seemed off that Clotile would point Mimi out to Sadie when the woman came into Lisette's that morning. And that's exactly what she'd done. That seemed irrational, drawing attention to someone who she knew was about to die. In fact, why would she even suggest meeting there?

"None of this makes sense, Coco." Sadie set her bottle of sparkling water down on a tile coaster decorated with a fleur-de-lis design. Coco returned a blank stare and then tapped her food bowl with her paw.

"What about Bluette?" Sadie said aloud as she began to pace. "I don't think the police have even bothered to investigate her, yet she would stand to gain by having her competition close." Sadie mulled that over. She'd only seen Bluette a couple of times, and both times the bakery owner had seemed quiet and preoccupied. Maybe she was being quiet in order to keep a low profile because she was guilty. She'd have to bring this up with Broussard.

Sadie flopped down on the bed, tired of running scenarios over and over in her head. It was exhausting. She'd intended the trip to be a vacation, not an episode of *Murder She Wrote*.

A clinking sound brought Sadie out of her reverie. Glancing at Coco, she was both dismayed and impressed to find that Coco had pushed her Villeroy and Boch bowl over to the side of her luxury kennel in order to tap the china against the metal wire of the siding.

"I'm sorry, Coco," Sadie said. "I guess I'm preoccupied. I forgot you didn't have the advantage of appetizers to fill you up before dinner."

Again, Coco tapped her paw on the food dish, clearly uninterested in excuses.

"How about chicken tonight?" Sadie opened a can of the Yorkie's favorite and filled the china bowl with a generous serving. Ten minutes later, Coco had finished her meal and curled up for an evening siesta.

Never should have said "chicken," Sadie thought to herself as her stomach rumbled. Perhaps the appetizers weren't enough to get through the night. She put on gold metallic flats, grabbed her wallet, and slipped out of the room. Making sure the door was locked behind her, she headed to the front desk.

The lobby was sparsely populated now, the wine-and-appetizer hour long over. A twenty-something male desk clerk replaced his expression of boredom with one of hospitality as Sadie approached the counter.

"I noticed a tiny chicken shack when I checked in, two doors down from here," Sadie ventured. "Can you tell me if it's any good?"

"Only good?" The young man smiled. Sadie could tell he was holding back a chuckle out of courtesy. She should have known better than to ask. She already knew from years of traveling that the smallest places often featured the best local fare.

"Do they prepare food to go?" Sadie asked. "And what do you recommend?"

The young clerk nodded. "Yes, in fact, they'll deliver right here to the lobby. They're fast too. We can charge it to your room." As for *what* to order, you don't have a choice." He laughed. "And you won't want one. Their fried chicken with butter beans, fried okra, and cornbread is out of this world. Would you like me to call it in for you?"

"That would be wonderful!" Sadie said. She watched while the clerk called in the order for "one plate" and then took a seat in an overstuffed armchair. In a matter of minutes, the food arrived. Sadie tipped the delivery person and headed back to her room, foil-covered plate balanced on one hand.

"Coco," Sadie called as she entered the room and relocked the door. "You're not the only one who gets chicken tonight." She set the dinner delivery down in the front room and kicked off her flats. "I might even share some with you."

Wishing she'd thought to order sweet tea, she headed to the refrigerator for bottled water but then froze as a shockwave of fear shot through her.

Coco's fancy travel palace was gone.

And so was Coco.

TWENTY

"**D**etective Broussard, please!"

"Ma'am, please try to calm down," the woman answering the phone at the police station said. "I'm trying to help you."

"Then get Detective Broussard for me!" Sadie wailed. "Tell him Coco has been dognapped!" She paced back and forth, trying not to hyperventilate. Fainting would do nothing to help the situation.

"Have you checked with the front desk of the hotel you're staying at?"

Sadie pounded her fist against her forehead. She couldn't possibly explain. She had to reach Broussard directly. "I can't," she said. "I just need to talk to Detective Broussard. Please, you have to find him!"

A sharp knock on the door interrupted the phone call. Clutching the phone to her chest, Sadie ran to the door's peephole and looked through it.

"Thank you!" she shouted to the woman on the phone.

"I'm not sure I…"

Sadie dropped the phone and flung open the door. She grabbed Detective Broussard by the sleeve and pulled him into her room. Under different circumstances, the action might have seemed inappropriate. But she was operating solely on panic.

"Ma'am…" The crackling voice was barely audible and not

at all to Sadie.

Detective Broussard guided Sadie to a chair and gently encouraged her to sit. "We're going to help," he said. "Just take a deep breath and tell me what happened."

"Ma'am? Ma'am?"

The detective picked Sadie's wayward phone up off the floor. "It's okay, Ruby. I'll take it from here." He set the phone down on a side table and turned back to Sadie.

"All I did was order chicken!" Sadie cried, her words barely understandable between hysterical sobs.

Broussard glanced at the foil package. "Best chicken in New Orleans too," he said. "Don't worry, it will be good later."

"I don't care about the chicken." Sadie sobbed. "I mean, seriously, Detective! Who likes fried okra anyway?"

"Well, actually…" Broussard started to speak but stopped as the two officers who'd helped with the first break-in approached from the hallway. "Here we go, Ms. Kramer. I think this will ease your fears."

Sadie looked up, discouraged but feeling a sense of anticipation grow after hearing Broussard's words. The first officer walked in, a pad of paper in one hand, a pen in the other. Sadie's spirits fell, and she slumped back in the chair. But when the second officer entered, she jumped up, hardly able to believe her eyes. In one hand he held a battered rendition of Coco's travel palace. In the other, he held Coco herself.

"Coco!" Sadie shouted, rushing to take the Yorkie from the officer. Coco showed equal enthusiasm, reaching for Sadie at first sight and covering her face with sloppy kisses once firmly secure in Sadie's arms.

"How? What?" Sadie had dozens of questions but found herself lacking the ability to verbalize them. All she wanted to do was hug Coco tight. Coco obviously reciprocated the feelings, as she cradled her petite canine head against Sadie's neck.

"Why don't you two relax a minute while I talk to the officers," Broussard said. "I'll be right back to explain what happened."

Sadie nodded, not taking her eyes off Coco for even a split second. Broussard left Sadie and Coco to rest and stepped outside the door. A muffled conversation ensued, of which Sadie heard not a word. Cuddling Coco was far more important.

After a few minutes, Broussard and the officers stepped back inside the room.

"Ms. Kramer," Broussard began, only to be stopped by Sadie.

"Just call me Sadie."

"All right," Broussard agreed. "Sadie, you must have questions."

"Well," Sadie said, realizing she had calmed down enough to gather her thoughts. "Yes, I do. Aside from the obvious— who took Coco, and why—I'm wondering how you got here so quickly. I'd barely started speaking to that woman on the phone…"

"The dispatcher," Broussard clarified. "She takes calls and relays them to us or to whichever department is appropriate."

Sadie nodded, wondering what this tidbit of information had to do with her question. "How is it you were here almost immediately? Or maybe it *was* immediately?" Suddenly she felt nervous again. Was something wrong with the whole picture? Could she not even trust the police? Again, nothing made sense. Broussard must have picked up on her confused thoughts, as he spoke to reassure her.

"We were already here, at least in a sense."

Sadie frowned. "Not to be repetitive, but that makes no sense."

"We witnessed the crime take place, so we were here before you called the station."

"Then why did I even have to call the station?" Sadie asked. "And how did you even know to be here in order to witness the crime?"

"I'm not explaining this well," Broussard said. "We witnessed the crime through the webcam that we've had trained on your door. We've been prepared to rush here since we installed the camera, hoping to catch whoever is behind this."

"So you caught him?" Sadie said, overlooking the comment about the camera. "You must have since you brought Coco back." She gave Coco a kiss on the top of her head and then wiped her mouth. The effects of the shower she'd given Coco recently had been erased by the dog's recent activity.

"Not exactly," Broussard admitted.

Sadie was trying to follow, but so far the story was confusing.

"The culprit fled into the alley and was in the process of removing the dog from the kennel when we called out for him to freeze."

"Then you did catch him," Sadie said.

Broussard shook his head. "No, unfortunately. The culprit dropped the kennel and took off on a bicycle that was parked by the alley fence. We think he planned to take the dog with him on the bike but panicked when we called out."

"We went in pursuit, but being on foot is no match for a bike," one of the officers said.

"There was no way to know the person had a bike stashed in the alley," Broussard said. "We did get a brief look at the bike, so we'll try to track that down. But it's a weak lead."

"Did you get a look at the person?" Sadie said, hoping at least they had a description.

Again, Broussard shook his head. "I wish we had. All we know is that the person was of medium height, wearing dark clothes and a hooded jacket or sweatshirt."

"Not much to go on," Sadie admitted.

"No," Broussard admitted. "But the hotel may have a security camera for the back alley. We'll find out."

"Okay," Sadie said. Still overwhelmed with relief that Coco's dognapping had been foiled, she only half followed the conversation.

"Don't worry. We'll stay on top of this," Broussard said. "If this is all tied in with Mimi Arnaud's murder, finding the person who tried to kidnap your dog tonight may lead us straight to the killer."

Somehow Sadie did not find that reassuring, as it implied the killer had been in her room. Twice, even, if the whipped cream episode was pulled off by the same person.

"Why don't you try to rest now," Broussard said. "That person isn't going to come back, knowing we arrived that quickly. He or she will know we have surveillance on your room."

"Relaxing does sound like a good idea," Sadie said. "I suddenly feel exhausted." She walked the detective and policemen to the door. Coco leaned sideways, sniffing the foil-covered plate that Sadie had set by the door.

"Thank you," Sadie said. She started to close the door but called Broussard back one more time. "Surveillance?" She asked. "You mean, like a camera? Where?" She twisted her head from side to side. Coco did the same, mimicking her movements.

Broussard looked around, as if pretending not to know,

and then glanced around the courtyard. He turned back to Sadie. "We have our ways."

"I see," Sadie said.

Broussard smiled and tipped an imaginary hat. "Good night."

TWENTY-ONE

Sadie twitched her nose to stifle a sneeze and then exhaled sharply, hoping to blow a tuft of fur out of her face.

Coco stirred upon feeling the burst of air but then settled back into the comfortable position she'd assumed the night before: upside down on Sadie's chest, three legs sticking up in the air, and the fourth resting against Sadie's face.

Multiple attempts late the previous evening had failed to convince Coco to enter her damaged kennel. Stubbornly she'd refused to have anything to do with the mangled mess that had been her travel palace. She even batted Sadie's hands away when she attempted to help her inside, which was highly out of character for her refined personality.

Sadie understood. Coco had her pride, after all, and the condition of the former housing known as a travel palace was poor by any standards, human or canine. The metal siding was dented, the silk interior lining was torn, and the velvet pillow was embedded with dirt and gravel. Perhaps worst of all, the china dishes were smashed to bits. Coco had been especially fond of those bowls, and Sadie doubted she'd be able to replace them with the same pattern.

"Coco," Sadie said. "You need to let me up. We can't sleep all morning."

Coco stretched, giving Sadie hope that she'd be able to slide out of bed and at least search out a cup of coffee. Instead, Coco rolled over on her stomach, draping her two front legs over one side of Sadie's body and her two back legs over the other.

"Sorry, my dear," Sadie said as she scooped Coco up off her chest and set her on the bed. "As pleasant as it was having your fur in my face all night, I'm determined to find some caffeine now. You can sleep later." She watched Coco roll onto her back and wiggle back and forth happily, which brought up a disturbing question: Would the Yorkie ever be content now sleeping on anything other than six-hundred-thread-count Egyptian sheets? Would replacing the velvet pillow not be enough? Perhaps Sadie would have to provide both.

Setting aside the predicament of Coco's housing, Sadie turned her mind to more pressing matters. She hadn't heard from Clotile since meeting her at Bluette's the day before. That didn't surprise her. Clotile was well aware of Sadie's distrust now. It came as no surprise that she hadn't received a text about meeting for breakfast, as had been Clotile's habit on other mornings. And Sadie wasn't about to contact her.

Looking through the remaining outfits she'd yet to wear, Sadie chose red jean-style pants and a red-and-white-striped blouse. Adding a chunky necklace that she'd picked up years ago at an art fair, she brushed her hair back from her face and dusted it with a quick spritz of hair spray.

"I need to find some crawfish earrings," she said to Coco. "Or something symbolic of New Orleans to take back with me." Lacking anything of that description at the moment, she rummaged through the jewelry she'd brought and clipped on a pair of dangling red pom-poms.

"Coffee, Coco. Let's go on a coffee hunt."

Less enthused than Sadie about leaving the luxurious bedding, Coco still allowed herself to be scooped up and placed in the tote bag. At least that hadn't changed since the day before, Sadie thought with relief. Coco did seem to enjoy traveling even if only for a few blocks. There was always a chance of something new to see or smell or, if lucky, to eat.

Sadie locked the room carefully though the thought crossed her mind to wonder why. Based on recent events, her hotel suite was hardly a secure fortress. It seemed easy enough for people to get in. At least Detective Broussard and his officers had a good eye on the place. She looked inside her bag and patted Coco's head, grateful that the police had quickly stopped the dognapping episode.

Heading up to the cluster of shops along Bourbon Street, Sadie specifically avoided the side of the street Bluette's was on, unsure if Clotile would be at the café that morning. Whether the woman would be by herself or seated with others, she wasn't in the mood for more complications. There was enough she already hadn't figured out.

The lure of fresh-brewed coffee came close to pulling her into several doorways, yet she kept walking. In spite of her intentions to stay away from Bluette's, she soon found herself on the same block. She was about to duck inside a hole-in-the-wall coffee place when she heard her name called out.

"Sadie? It's Sadie, right?"

Looking around, she spotted Lisette sweeping the sidewalk in front of Chez Lisette Patisserie. Delighted to see her out and about, Sadie walked over to say hello.

"Yes, it's Sadie," she said, reaching out to shake hands with Lisette. "Are you open again?" Sadie surveyed the front of the bakery, noting a closed doorway and the absence of lights. "Ah, I guess not. I'm sorry."

"It's okay," Lisette said. "I'm getting ready to open the day after tomorrow. It's just taken some time to clean up."

"I can imagine," Sadie said. "I came by while the police were here the other day. They were doing a thorough job going through everything. I'm sure that left a mess."

"Yes, and when they finished, all those supplies had to be thrown out," Lisette said.

Sadie picked up on a tinge of discouragement in the bakery owner's voice, but overall she seemed ready to put Mimi Arnaud's awful demise behind her and to go forward with business.

"Come on in," Lisette said.

"But you're not open." Sadie glanced at a Closed sign in the window.

"No, but I do have coffee brewing. I'm not about to do all this work without caffeine," Lisette said. "I don't have anything to go with it since Julien doesn't start back until tomorrow."

"Just coffee sounds great," Sadie said, realizing she had yet to even partially caffeinate herself. Admittedly, one of Lisette's beignets would have been fabulous with the cup of java, but she'd just have to wait until the bakery reopened.

"Wow," Sadie said as she followed Lisette. "Your place looks immaculate!" Tables and chairs sat neatly stacked on one side of the room. The floor had been buffed and polished to a perfect shine. The display cases were so clean they appeared to be brand-new.

At Lisette's direction, Sadie followed her to the back. The area was just as impressive as the front. Shelves stood empty yet scrubbed down and ready to hold new supplies. Cases of ingredients rested unopened along the wall. And the work area floor itself was polished to perfection.

"Neat and clean, just like the front," Sadie observed.

"Now, that took some doing, I'll tell you," Lisette said. She leaned the broom against a wall and poured Sadie a mug of freshly brewed coffee. "I don't know what the police did back here when they tested the ingredients. There was flour everywhere! It was such a mess!"

Sadie cleared her throat nervously and then took a sip of coffee.

"Anyway, it's finally cleaned up," Lisette continued. "Julien will organize the supplies tomorrow to prepare for baking tomorrow night. I'll set up the front and get the display cases ready to fill. Thank goodness the police released Julien right after questioning him. I could never get this place open on my own. Good pastry chefs are hard to find too."

"Are you nervous about reopening after… everything that happened?" Sadie asked, hoping she didn't sound intrusive.

"Yes and no," Lisette admitted. "I know there will be questions, and I expect business to be down even though we've been cleared."

Sadie nodded, understanding. "I noticed it's been busy across the street. That must be tough to watch."

"Over at Bluette's place? I don't mind that at all," Lisette said. "I'm happy to see her get some extra business."

"You are?" Sadie said, quickly realizing how abrupt that sounded. "I mean…"

Lisette laughed. "I know what you mean. Everyone thinks we're in competition with each other, but we really aren't. We've known each other since grade school. We're friends. If there's any competition, it's friendly competition. What one business does helps the other."

Sadie thought that over. It was true with her fashion boutique business too. She often sent customers to other shops, and they sent customers to her, as well.

"I know it will take time to build up our clientele again," Lisette continued. "That part will be a challenge. But it also feels like a new beginning, with everything spick-and-span."

"Makes sense," Sadie said. "I'm glad we'll still be here in town to see you reopen. We go back to San Francisco the next day."

"We?" Lisette said.

A timely *yip* came from the tote bag.

"Ah, yes, of course." Lisette laughed. "Would you like to let her out?"

Sadie eyed a sack of flour against the wall. "Thanks, but I'd better not. She can be a little wild at times. Doesn't always understand the word *no*." A tiny snort that only Sadie could hear followed that statement.

"Oh, you haven't happened to hear from Clotile, have you?" Lisette said. "I haven't heard from her while we've been closed. I hope she's okay."

The subject change took Sadie by surprise. She certainly wasn't going to fill Lisette in on recent developments, especially when she wasn't even sure which parts of Clotile's story were true and which weren't.

"Not today," Sadie said, avoiding a more detailed response. "But if I hear from her, I'll tell her you asked about her." She finished her coffee and looked around for a place to put the mug.

"Thanks," Lisette said, taking the mug and putting it in a side sink. "I'm sure she'll be at the reopening."

"I'm sure you're right," Sadie said. "She'll be here." *Or maybe not,* she added to herself before continuing. "I'll let you get back to work. I can tell Coco is getting restless. I'd better take her for a walk. Thanks so much for the coffee."

"Anytime," Lisette said as she picked up the broom she'd set aside earlier. "And the day after tomorrow you can have beignets with it."

"That's a deal," Sadie said.

Once outside, Sadie attached Coco's rhinestone leash to her matching collar and started the walk back to the hotel. She hadn't learned much, but she'd picked up a few bits of information. A trip to see Detective Broussard was in order.

TWENTY-TWO

S adie waited patiently in the reception area of the police station while the desk clerk summoned Detective Broussard. When Broussard emerged from the back, he invited Sadie to his office. He closed the door while she took a seat.

"You wanted to see me," he said, stating the obvious. After all, she'd been the one to call and ask to stop by.

"Yes," Sadie said. "I was just at Chez Lisette Patisserie. They're reopening the day after tomorrow. Isn't that fabulous? I'm just dying for one of her beignets."

"Probably not the best choice of words," Broussard suggested.

"Oh!" Sadie said, wishing she could take the words back. "No, I guess not. I wasn't thinking. Anyway, that's not what I came to tell you."

"I was hoping there might be more," Broussard said.

Sadie nodded. "There is. Lisette and I got to talking about Bluette's Beignets. You know the bakery across the street where we met the other day."

"Go on," Broussard said.

"The topic of competition came up," Sadie said. "After all, they're right across the street from each other. I'm sure you've considered competition as a motive."

"Only mildly," Broussard said. "It's not a strong motive for something as extreme as murder. There are less drastic ways to attract business from a competitive company."

"True," Sadie said. "But I thought you'd want to know Lisette made it very clear the competition between them is friendly. It turns out they've known each other since grade school."

"Well, that clears that up then," Broussard said, smiling.

Sadie huffed. "You're not taking me seriously."

"I assure you I am," Broussard said. "Every potential motive has to be considered, no matter how unlikely it might be. We do ourselves a disservice if we write something off as not important before making sure it isn't."

"Well, now you know for sure that competition isn't a factor," Sadie said, certain she'd done a great service to the police by discovering the rivalry between the two was more for show than anything else.

"Thank you," Broussard said.

"Will you be at the reopening?" Sadie said. "Lisette's done such a beautiful job fixing the place up. Made me think about the remodeling the hotel is planning."

Broussard leaned forward. "What remodeling?"

"The hotel is planning to remodel," Sadie said. "At least I think it is."

"Why do you think that?"

"I saw Horace LeBlanc drop a paper at Bluette's the other day," Sadie said. "I picked it up. It's not appropriate to litter, you know." She shook her head with an expression of disapproval.

"Yet you kept the paper instead of throwing it in the trash, as someone would do with litter," Broussard pointed out. "And you also didn't catch up to the man who dropped it, to give it back to him."

Sadie shrugged her shoulders. "I was curious. Horace and the other man had been going over the papers when Clotile came in and started arguing with them.

"Clotile is the friend you met on the plane coming here. She was with you at the bakery that morning."

"Yes," Sadie said. "Also… Horace makes me nervous. He could be involved, you know. There's a family feud that goes way back. You should look into that."

"We're looking into many possibilities," Broussard said. "But let's back up a minute. You kept the paper but didn't think it was important to bring it to our attention here at the station, is that correct?"

"After I got back to the hotel room and looked at the paper, I figured they were just arguing about the remodeling plans," Sadie said. "People often disagree with things like that, you know—wallpaper, for instance, or whether or not to have statues of lions at the front entrance, or if they should—"

"Yes, I see your point," Broussard said quickly.

"I didn't think it would matter," Sadie said.

Broussard leveled a gaze at Sadie. "Everything matters until we say it doesn't. Do you still have it?"

"Yes. In fact, I think I have it with me." Sadie rummaged through her bag, much to Coco's annoyance. Eventually she found the paper stuffed in an inside pocket. She pulled it out and handed it to the detective.

"You say this is a plan for remodeling?" Broussard looked over the paper, frowning. "I'm not so sure about that."

"Look at the diagrams," Sadie said. "You can see that one section is shaped like the lobby. So I figured it must be remodeling or renovating or something like that. What else do you think it is?" Coco stuck her head out of the tote bag, appearing to be interested in the answer, as well.

"You see the notes at the bottom of the page and those initials?" Broussard pointed out a small section of writing.

"This was put together by some sort of business entity. There's no address, but there's a phone number." He contemplated the paper, thinking. "Looks like a Chicago area code."

Sadie shrugged her shoulders. "I don't know what that's supposed to mean."

"I can tell you what it means," Broussard said as he stood up. "It means I need to make a phone call. Wait here." He left the room, taking the diagram and notes with him.

Sadie watched the detective leave the room, closing the door behind him. With no idea how long he would be gone, she took Coco out of the tote and set her down on the floor. Coco stretched her front legs, then her back, and proceeded to cruise around the perimeter of the room. Apparently, Broussard was not the only one who considered himself a detective. Coco was determined to sniff out whatever she might find.

Ten minutes passed and then another ten. Finally Broussard returned to the room. He carried a legal size notepad with half a page of scribbled writing on it. His hand gripped a pen.

"What did you find out?" Sadie asked, as if they were equal partners in getting to the bottom of whatever was going on with the hotel, the Arnaud and LeBlanc families, and the odd cast of peripheral characters. Of course, there were those pesky details too: the tainted whipped cream showing up in her fridge and the recent dognapping episode.

"I can't comment on an ongoing investigation." Broussard sat down and looked at Sadie. "We'll need to keep the paper."

"I figured you'd hold on to it," Sadie said.

"The notations at the bottom may help us. And we'll run it for fingerprints and see what comes back."

"Obviously you'll find mine since I just handed it to you," Sadie said. "And Horace LeBlanc's will be on there. And probably Clotile's since she tapped something during that argument. Oh, and maybe a paw print…"

This last thought reminded Sadie that Coco was still loose. She glanced around the room and then under the table, where she found Coco polishing the unsuspecting detective's shoes with kisses. She called Coco over to her before Broussard noticed. Placing her back in the tote, she turned her attention back to the discussion at hand.

"I hope the paper helps you," Sadie said. "It's the least I can do in exchange for protecting me with pruning shears."

"Uh… sure," Broussard said. He frowned and then stood up. Sadie followed his lead, and the two walked to the front of the station.

"Maybe we'll find something; maybe we won't," Broussard said. "We won't know until we check. I wouldn't worry about the paw print. I doubt it will be in our system." He paused for a moment. "Or will it?"

"Of course not!" Sadie bristled at the implication, though she suspected the detective wasn't being serious.

"Good," Broussard said. "I'll be in touch then."

Sadie thanked him and walked outside.

"Silly me," Sadie said to Coco. "I shouldn't have mentioned your paw print—or their surveillance techniques, for that matter. They do need their secrets, after all."

The yip from her tote bag confirmed this. That was one nice thing about Coco. She always agreed.

TWENTY-THREE

CCC 5:00?

Sadie didn't know whether she should be concerned that she knew what the text meant or not. She was a few decades too old for teen text abbreviations, but she understood Clotile's question nonetheless.

Sounds good.

It did sound good, after all. Happy hour at Cyril's was one of the better late afternoon hot spots she'd ever been to, at least from the food and drink viewpoint. And she was determined to take in as much New Orleans culture as she could before heading back to San Francisco—great food, great music, and great people-watching opportunities. There was no doubt about it. Cyril's Crazy Cajun Cookery had it all.

Arriving early, Sadie had her choice of a few tables. She grabbed one not far from the buffet, openly admitting to herself that the table's proximity to food made it especially appealing. She ordered a Hurricane from the server and then helped herself to a selection of sausage-stuffed mushrooms and crab fingers. She returned to her table just as the Hurricane arrived. Sitting back, she sipped her drink, dipped a crab finger in cocktail sauce, and waited for Clotile to arrive. Before long, half her Hurricane was gone and her foot was tapping along with the music.

"Diggy Liggy Lo!"

Sadie watched Clotile slide into the seat across from her.

"What did you say?" She'd recognized the voice but not the words.

"Diggy Liggy Lo," Clotile repeated as she waved to the server and pointed to Sadie's drink. Turning back to Sadie, she said, "Diggy Liggy Lo…"

"Clotile! Stop it!" Sadie laughed. "I don't speak any foreign languages."

Clotile glanced under the table and then back at Sadie. "Well, your foot does. I was trying to tell you that's the name of the song. It's a favorite Cajun tune."

"Oh," Sadie said. "Of course. I knew that."

Clotile rolled her eyes. "Right."

"It's nice to see you out of disguise," Sadie said, earning a return look that was either amused or annoyed. Most likely, it was both.

"I didn't want to take a chance of being recognized," Clotile said.

Sadie took a sip of her drink and set it down. "I'd say that was obvious. People don't usually wear disguises for any other reason."

"Good point," Clotile said. She paid the server as her drink arrived, then she headed to the buffet. She returned with the same assortment of appetizers that Sadie had chosen. "Can't go wrong with crab fingers," she said.

"Back to the disguise," Sadie said.

"Oh, that," Clotile said. "Really, it was silly. I was just being paranoid, I guess."

"Paranoid?" Sadie almost choked on a stuffed mushroom. "You scared the heck out of me, saying we were both in danger. And then I didn't hear from you after that."

"I'm sorry," Clotile said. "I ran into… an old friend the other day. Well, not exactly a friend. Someone from my past,"

Clotile said. "It doesn't matter now."

"Well, it matters to me." Sadie leaned closer and cupped her hand in such a way that her words wouldn't reach her tote bag. "Someone tried to steal Coco last night."

"What?" Clotile's stunned look appeared sincere. "Why didn't you call me?" She paused. "Oh wait, I get it. Now you think I did that too? Just like you accused me of trying to poison you?" She looked around the room and then back at Sadie. "So where is he?"

"Who?"

"The detective," Clotile said. "Do you have a detective with you again? Is that why you agreed to meet me here?" She stood up, ready to walk out.

"Sit back down," Sadie said, swishing her hand in the air as if to brush the tension away. "There's no detective here with me. I agreed to meet you because I wanted to."

Clotile looked dubious but also eyed the drink and appetizers she was about to abandon. "Fine," she said. She sat back down and picked up a crab finger.

"But I want you to tell me what's going on, Clotile," Sadie said. "You know more than you're saying. You can't tell me we're in danger and then not tell me why. Or at least tell me why you said that."

Clotile took a hearty slug of her drink and leaned forward. "Listen, you can't repeat this, or we *will* be in danger."

Sadie remained quiet, waiting.

"I ran into Johnny the other day," Clotile said. "A guy from my past. I worked with him on a few deals but got out when I realized he was involved in some bad business."

"Where was this?" Sadie asked.

"In Chicago."

Sadie froze. *Chicago?*

"You're from Chicago? Are you working with LMNOP?" Sadie watched Clotile closely.

"Am I *what?*"

"I asked if you're working with LMNOP," Sadie said.

"How many Hurricanes have you had?" Clotile asked, incredulous. "What kind of name is LMNOP?"

"A ridiculous one, but forget that for now," Sadie said. After all, she wasn't going to get a straight answer anyway. "You never mentioned Chicago before. I thought you were a local." Sadie fought to keep her voice steady. What was it about this vacation that had her constantly in fight-or-flight mode?

"I *am* a local!" Clotile said. "I was born here, right down the street at Charity Hospital, the one that closed after Katrina. My family goes back generations. My name is *Clotile Laurent*, for heaven's sake. Does that sound like a good old Chicago name to you?"

Sadie considered it. "You could be from Quebec or Paris."

"Or Montreal or the Côte d'Azur," Clotile added. "But I'm not."

"Fine," Sadie said. "Tell me who this 'Johnny' is." *The man at the French Market, the man in the alley, and the man talking with Horace, These things I already know.* She kept these thoughts to herself, once again feeling she couldn't trust anyone, including Clotile.

"I need more crab fingers first," Clotile said.

"Totally understandable," Sadie said. She followed Clotile to the buffet. When they returned, Clotile launched into her story.

"I met Johnny at a bar called Tony's. I'd just moved up to Chicago and was looking for work. Johnny bought me a drink and told me he was into real estate and needed someone to work in the office, an administrative assistant."

"A pickup line if I ever heard one," Sadie quipped.

"Exactly what I thought!" Clotile said, completely missing Sadie's sarcasm. "But I needed a job, so I visited the office. Everything seemed on the up-and-up, so I started working."

Sadie downed the rest of her Hurricane. "If I could make that scary sound that precedes danger in slapstick films now, I would."

"Dun, dun, dun," Clotile mimicked.

"Close enough," Sadie said.

The server stopped by the table for drink reorders. Clotile ordered another, but Sadie declined. She needed to be able to think clearly in order to tell Clotile's truths from her lies. Something wasn't adding up. The question was what.

"It didn't take long to figure out Johnny was up to no good," Clotile said. "He was running real estate scams, taking advantage of people."

Sadie knew about real estate deals from her late husband's business. There were good deals, there were bad deals, and there were *really* bad deals. It sounded like Johnny was into the latter, and the Hotel Arnaud-LeBlanc was about to be a victim of his schemes. That didn't bode well for Horace, who obviously knew something was wrong by now. Sadie thought back to the conversation she'd overheard in the alley. *"You shouldn't have come here... It's none of your business... I'm making it my business now..."*

"So that's why you were arguing with Horace and Johnny?"

Clotile blinked. "What are you talking about?"

Sadie waited for the server to set Clotile's drink order down and walk away before continuing. "I was at Bluette's the other morning when you walked in and approached their table, Clotile," Sadie said. "I saw how angry you were. Not to mention the smug looks on their faces after you walked out."

"Smug looks? Well, of all the nerve." Clotile grabbed her Hurricane and gulped a third of it down. A new Cajun tune sounded from the overhead speakers. "'Jolie Blonde'!" Clotile clapped her hands. "Another good one."

"Focus, Clotile!" Sadie said.

"I am focusing," Clotile said, drink in hand and head swinging side to side with the beat of the music. "On the song and the Hurricane."

Her patience growing thinner, Sadie decided to try a different approach.

"I have a copy of the papers Horace and Johnny were looking at."

Clotile's party attitude screeched to a hot Cajun halt. "What? You have the papers?"

"I have one," Sadie said. "Horace dropped it on his way out of Bluette's. That's how I know about LMNOP. So don't try to tell me you don't know what it is. That's the company you worked for in Chicago, isn't it?"

Clotile shook her head. "No. Johnny had a few companies. Actually, a different one for each deal. SMNYP, for example, and RMLAP."

"What did those stand for?" Sadie asked.

"Let me think," Clotile said. "Not that I want to remember those deals. With the SMNYP deal, the building just happened to burn down right before the deal closed. And with RMLAP, a water main broke. That was a mess. So much damage…"

"The initials, Clotile," Sadie prompted.

"SMNYP… that was for Stevens-Malone New York Properties," Clotile said. "And let me think… RMLAP was for Rogers-Malone Los Angles Properties."

"Johnny's last name is Malone, isn't it?" Sadie said.

Clotile nodded. "Yes, John Malone. He always bragged

about being related to Bugsy Malone. You know…"

"That should have been a sign right there," Sadie pointed out.

Clotile sighed. "I figured that out. Just not soon enough."

"It doesn't matter now. We need to warn Horace," Sadie said. "And call Detective Broussard too.

"Because…" Clotile knowingly allowed Sadie to finish.

"Because LMNOP stands for LeBlanc-Malone New Orleans Properties."

TWENTY-FOUR

Horace was nowhere to be found when Sadie and Clotile reached the hotel. The front desk clerk could only offer that "he stepped out unexpectedly."

That did not sit well with Sadie. One murder was enough for one vacation. Besides, who would another victim be if there were to be one? Horace—because Johnny was fed up with him? Johnny—because Horace was fed up with *him*? Clotile—because she blew Johnny's cover when she argued with him at the bakery that day? Back to Horace—because Clotile exposed Johnny's background in running scams? Or, could it be...

No, she wasn't even going to think it could be herself. Everything they'd done so far seemed intended to scare her away. The whipped cream switch had happened quickly while she was taking Coco for a walk. An anonymous tip was called into the police immediately. She wouldn't have found the whipped cream in that short a time. That was a setup.

And stealing Coco? No, it was unthinkable that whoever was behind this would harm a sweet, innocent dog. That was intended to scare her as well. Who would try to steal a large travel palace on a bicycle? They might have even intended to drop it in the alley and drive away. That alone would have given her a scare—an understatement for sure—when she would have found her in the alley.

Any one of these people might have been the one to

kill Mimi. Like everything else, the question was why. She still couldn't figure out a motive. No one had said anything negative about Mimi. Besides, she ran the hotel. She was valuable, an asset. Again, there was no motive that she could figure.

Sadie stepped away from the desk but paused at the reader board, which listed special events at the hotel via a digital printout. Dignified wording announced "Mimi Arnaud Celebration of Life—7:00 P.M. in the Gallery Room."

"Clotile," Sadie said, thinking she was standing right beside her. Instead, she had to look around the lobby. She finally found her in a far corner, reading a fashion magazine.

"Did you see that board by the front desk, the one with announcements?" Sadie asked. "It says there's a celebration of life here tonight for Mimi Arnaud."

Clotile shrugged her shoulders. "That makes sense. She ran this place, you know."

"True." Sadie agreed. "Oh, and Horace is gone."

Clotile looked up from an article on hairstyles. "What do you mean *gone?*"

"I mean he's not here," Sadie said. "The front desk said he stepped out unexpectedly. Don't you find that odd?"

"Not really," Clotile replied. "He's been gone for years. I think it's strange he's here at all even if he is working on some real estate deal. Johnny always prefers to work on his own. He feels owners get in the way of his methods."

"I would imagine so," Sadie said. "According to what you've told me of his past deals. Speaking of which, I need to give Broussard an update. Maybe I should go alone." Sadie mentally crossed her fingers, hoping Clotile would agree to this. It would be easier to talk to the detective alone.

"Great idea," Clotile said. "I have other things to do anyway."

"What other things?" Sadie said, her suspicions taking yet another unexpected turn. *A person could get dizzy switching suspects this often*, she thought to herself.

Clotile sent her a frustrated look, as if reading her mind. "Look, if you want to think I'm guilty multiple times per day, go ahead." She slapped the magazine down on a lobby table and stood up. "I've told you everything I know. You can believe me or not. I don't care at this point. Do what you want. I'm going to help Lisette get ready for the bakery's reopening." She stormed off in a huff.

"Well!" Sadie said to Coco. "I'd say everyone's on edge, wouldn't you? I suppose I need to count myself in there too." Sadie took the tentative yip that followed as proof. "Too much thinking and not enough action, that's the problem. Let's go talk to Broussard."

* * *

The police station was beginning to look far too familiar, especially for a vacation. There were plenty of other places in New Orleans that Sadie would have preferred to visit multiple times. Yet there she was again.

"Detective Broussard, please."

As confirmation of her multiple visits, the officer at the front desk had already picked up the phone to call the detective. "Someone is here to see you," she said, pausing. "Yes, it is."

"We're famous, Coco," Sadie said as she sat down to wait for Broussard. "Although, considering where we are, that could be 'infamous.'"

"Ms. Kramer," Broussard said as he emerged from the back. "What a surprise." His expression contradicted his words.

"I have new information for you," Sadie said.

"Come on back."

Sadie followed Broussard, though she wouldn't have had to. The station layout had become far too familiar to her. She was soon seated across from the detective.

"Go on," Broussard said.

What? No coffee this time? Maybe she was wearing out the welcome mat at this point.

"I know who the man is that Horace LeBlanc has been meeting with," Sadie said. "His name is John Malone, and he runs real estate scams." She sat back in her chair, pleased with herself. Perhaps they'd make her an honorary deputy or something. At least she could go back to San Francisco with a badge for a souvenir.

"We know who Johnny Malone is," Broussard said.

There goes my badge, Sadie thought. She just couldn't catch a break on this supposed vacation. Maybe she would consider some sort of Zen retreat for her next trip. At least it would be calmer with little chance of crime.

"Oh," Sadie said.

"Chicago PD keeps an eye on him because of shady real estate dealings," Broussard said.

"Yes," Sadie said. "I was going to tell you."

Broussard frowned. "How did you know that?"

Sadie stalled a moment, feeling a brief tug of questionable friendship for Clotile but knew she needed to divulge everything. After all, there was a killer to be caught.

"Clotile told me," Sadie said. "She knew Johnny when she lived in Chicago. She worked with him but quit when she realized he was running scams and taking advantage of people."

"I see," Broussard said as he jotted down notes on the pad of paper.

Sadie leaned forward in an attempt to read what the detective had written but pulled back when he shot her a look of disapproval.

"And Horace LeBlanc is away. According to the hotel front desk, he 'stepped out' unexpectedly," Sadie offered.

Broussard stopped writing. "Really? Now that, we didn't know."

Sadie sat back, a satisfied look on her face. *Maybe I'll get my badge after all.*

"Anything else?" Broussard leaned forward, ready to stand.

"Not at this time," Sadie said, impressed with how official she sounded.

"Then I have something I'd like you to look at," Broussard said. "Follow me."

"Sure," Sadie said, puzzled. She retrieved Coco, who was once again sniffing for clues around the room. "Aren't you curious, Coco?" She received a double yip in return. Clearly, Coco was just as curious as she was.

Broussard led Sadie down the hallway, back to a room with computers and screens.

"Have a seat," he said, indicating a chair in front of one monitor. Sadie sat down and waited for instructions.

"Run that tape," Broussard said to a young tech-type person at the computer. He turned back to Sadie. "I want you to watch carefully and tell me if you see anything of interest."

Sadie was surprised to see footage of the back alley behind the hotel appear on the screen. Although the film was a night scene, the silhouette of a person running into the alley was clear, as well as what the person was holding: Coco's travel palace.

Sadie gasped and then cringed when the figure dropped the kennel. The culprit ran a short distance, grabbed a bike that was leaning against the wall, and took off at a fast pace.

"We haven't been able to gain much from this hotel security tape," Broussard said. "Do you see anything we might be missing?"

"Aside from my poor Coco being dropped?" Sadie's voice wavered as she fought back tears. "No," she said, shaking her head. "I'm sorry. Seeing Coco treated like that was a shock. Can you play it again? I'll make a point of being more objective."

Broussard instructed the young technician to replay the footage. Sadie watched it a second time and asked to see it again. On the third time through, she sat up straight at one point and shouted, "Stop!" She asked the technician to enlarge it, which he did. Sadie leaned forward, inspecting the image in front of her, and then sat back, silent.

"Again?" Broussard asked, watching Sadie curiously.

Sadie shook her head.

"No," she said. "There's no need. I know who the killer is."

TWENTY-FIVE

Gathering her tote bag, Sadie exited the police station and stood on the front steps, debating her next move. The plan she'd worked out with Broussard could not be put into play until later that evening. She needed to kill some time.

As long as she was in such a helpful mode, she decided helping Lisette and Clotile prepare for the bakery's reopening would be a good use of her afternoon. She left the station and headed over to Lisette's.

Although the Closed sign hung in the window at Chez Lisette Patisserie, the front door was ajar. Sadie pushed it open, stepped inside, and repositioned the door as she'd found it.

"Sadie." Lisette looked up from behind the glass display cases. "How nice to see you."

The scene inside was not at all what Sadie expected. She'd envisioned a crowd of people working together, music in the background, a jovial sense of anticipation in the air as everyone helped Lisette prepare for the reopening. Instead, she found Lisette placing doilies on trays for the display cases.

"I just thought I'd stop in and help you and Clotile," Sadie said.

"Clotile?" Lisette looked confused. "I haven't seen her."

"Really," Sadie said. "You're here alone?"

"Julien is in the back putting the finishing touches on a sheet cake for Mimi Arnaud's reception," Lisette said. "It has to be delivered to the hotel soon." She pushed one doily-covered tray into the display case and pulled another out. "Did Clotile say she was coming by?"

"Yes," Sadie said. "We went to the hotel to look for Horace and then split up. I went to the police station to talk to Broussard. Clotile said she was going to come here."

Lisette shook her head. "Well, obviously she didn't. In fact, she'd been rather aloof since Mimi's… well, since that morning, aside from the night we all met up at Cyril's place. I hope she's okay." She waved a doily in the direction of a basket by the register. "Have a praline. I make those myself, so they're already wrapped and ready for customers."

Sadie understood Lisette's avoidance of the word *murder*. The bakery owner was ready to move on. Who wouldn't be, in her shoes? Meanwhile, she wasn't about to turn down one of Lisette's pralines.

Ironic, Sadie thought as she bit into the delicious pecan treat. Lisette's mouthwatering pralines were responsible for her falling into the whole Mimi Arnaud mess. Amazing the power a buttery brown sugar mixture could have.

"I definitely need to buy some of these to take back to San Francisco with me," Sadie said. "I was addicted from the first bite Clotile gave me on the flight here."

"They freeze well," Lisette said. She switched out another tray in the display case.

"Then I'll have to take a few dozen," Sadie said. "Is that too many?"

"Not at all," Lisette said. "I have plenty. I'll set them aside today."

Sadie finished off the praline and offered to help Lisette with the trays. Lisette readily accepted, and the two began to work side by side.

"I don't understand why Clotile isn't here," Sadie said. "I was sure she said…" Sadie's voice trailed off at the sound of footsteps approaching.

"I'm here," Clotile shouted as she stepped through the doorway. "I figured you could use some help, Lisette… and Sadie?" She dropped a purse and sweater on a table. "I thought you were going to talk to that detective."

"I did," Sadie said. "It didn't take long. I just filled him in. It's not like I'm joining the force you know." It suddenly occurred to her it might be an interesting career move on her part, but she quickly ruled it out. Not only would her Zen retreat be out of the question but she'd miss her fashion boutique too much, not to mention Matteo's constant supply of chocolate.

"Did you get things straightened out with the detective?" Clotile asked. She grabbed a stack of doilies and began to help fill the trays. Sadie could tell she was trying not to say too much in front of Lisette. And it was a safe bet she didn't want a detailed answer.

"Yes, as a matter of fact," Sadie said. "It was a very productive meeting."

"That's good, right?" Lisette said. "The sooner this whole thing is behind me, the happier I'll be. I'm ready to get back to business as usual."

"Of course you are, Lisette," Clotile said. "This whole thing has been dreadful for you. Not to mention the loss of business."

"It was only a few days," Lisette said. "I'll be fine." She went to the back to see how the cake was coming along. Pleased to find out it was finished and on the way to the hotel already, she returned to the front.

"Will you be at Mimi's gathering tonight, Lisette?" Sadie

asked as she set aside a finished tray.

"Of course," Lisette said. "Mimi was a lovely person, in addition to being a devoted customer. I wouldn't miss the opportunity to pay my respects."

Sadie glanced at Clotile. "You'll be there, won't you?"

Clotile nodded her head. "With free food and drinks? You bet. Er, I mean to pay my respects as well, of course."

Sadie and Lisette exchanged amused looks.

"I imagine just about everyone will be there," Clotile said. "Mimi had the respect of the hotel, as well as the community. She didn't have any enemies."

An odd thing to say about someone who was murdered, Sadie thought, although this now made sense to her.

"Yes," Lisette said. "I believe everyone who's anyone will be there."

Sadie looked at both women and smiled. It was exactly what she wanted to hear.

TWENTY-SIX

Sadie strolled through the Gallery Room, impressed. Lisette hadn't been exaggerating. Half of New Orleans must have shown up for Mimi Arnaud's Celebration of Life. Or perhaps it was Mimi's Celebration of Free Food and Wine that brought the crowds in. Whichever it was, it didn't matter. The people Sadie wanted there had all shown up.

"Lovely event, don't you think?"

Sadie turned to her side, where she found Clotile in a striking emerald-green dress that complemented her red hair perfectly. Clotile held up a glass of white wine and leaned over closer to Sadie. "No Hurricanes here, but the wine's not bad." She took a sip and wandered off to join Lisette at the buffet.

As much as Sadie hated to admit it, the event's food spread put Cyril's Crazy Cajun Cookery's Happy Hour to shame in comparison. Of course, this was a bigger event, with more sentimentality attached to it, so it was to be expected. Although Lisette's bakery had provided the cake—an elegant one, at that—the rest of the lavish buffet had been catered by Bluette's. This was to be expected since it was within the family. Horace LeBlanc, now sole owner of Hotel Armand-LeBlanc, would certainly order through his own niece's business.

Bluette herself, quiet as usual, continually replenished the buffet table. Whenever the hot crab dip or Cajun-spiced meatballs began to run low, she reached below the linen banquet tablecloth and brought out more. The sizable crystal bowl of cocktail sauce never lacked a circle of shrimp around the rim. Each time one was plucked from the edge by a guest, another appeared. Had Sadie not seen the chilled containers and heated thermal boxes being stocked below the table earlier, she might have thought Bluette capable of pulling crab cakes out of a magician's hat.

Sadie had purchased a new outfit for the occasion at a small boutique not far from the hotel. She'd only packed casual clothes for the trip, never anticipating attending a memorial celebration for someone she never even knew. But any excuse to shop was a good excuse in her book. Therefore she felt no guilt in picking up the rose-colored silk sheath and jacket, as well as a string of pearls to add a sophisticated touch to the attire. Not to leave Coco out, she'd picked up an extra strand of pearls for the Yorkie.

"You look quite lovely, Ms. Kramer."

Surprised to hear the compliment arrive cloaked in Broussard's voice, she paused before glancing at the detective, who pinned a carnation on her lapel.

"I suppose I won't be spouting any deep dark secrets or inappropriate jokes tonight," Sadie said, a knowing smirk on her face.

"Testing, testing," Broussard said, tilting his mouth in the direction of the floral accessory. "Entirely up to you," he said, smiling as he straightened up. "We all enjoy entertainment."

In a bold move that she knew couldn't show up on audio, she lightly elbowed the detective in his side.

Horace entered, dressed more formally than most others in the room.

"I wonder if he came from Mimi's funeral," Sadie murmured. She watched as Horace crossed to the buffet table and placed a kiss on Bluette's forehead before moving around the room to greet guests. His somber expression and the way a few of the older attendees patted him on the shoulder or even hugged him made her wonder. Were they worried about the burden he'd bear without Mimi to run the hotel or simply expressing polite condolences? Or was it something more?

"It seems we have all hands on deck," Broussard said, looking around the room.

"Yes," Sadie said. "It's a wonderful turnout. I think it's inspiring to see the way the hotel has pulled together for this tribute. The front desk, the housekeeping staff, and the gardeners are all here to make sure the hotel is at its best."

"How fortunate for us all," Broussard said. "I think I'll celebrate with one of those puff pastry concoctions that I saw when I passed by the buffet."

"Delicious!" Sadie said. "I tried one when Bluette first put them out. They're stuffed with Andouille sausage." An excited yip followed the word *sausage*, causing Broussard to frown. Sadie moved her tote away from the carnation, holding it in her hand, rather than keeping it on her shoulder.

Even Johnny Malone had shown up, much to Sadie's relief. He was the one person she'd counted on to arrive of his own accord—the one link she worried might be missing at the event. Instead of being a no-show, he'd been one of the first to arrive. He'd positioned himself not far from the buffet, a socially correct glass of wine in his hand, and a not-so-proper flask of something stronger hidden in a pocket. Admittedly, Sadie had flinched the first time he'd reached inside his jacket but relaxed when she saw him slyly pull out the container.

As the celebration continued, the celebrating intensified. Clotile compensated for the lack of Hurricanes by imbibing larger quantities of white wine. Lisette joined Bluette behind the buffet, the two working together to keep up with the ravenous crowd. Laughter increased exponentially, and strangers became friends as they admired a photo collage of Mimi's life and dedication to the hotel.

Even Horace seemed to relax, his expression softening as condolences continued to roll in. So when he picked up a spoon from the buffet and tapped it against his wineglass, a jovial crowd paused to hear what he had to say.

"We are here today to honor Mimi Arnaud's life," Horace said. Bluette reached up and patted her uncle's shoulder as he continued. "And I feel honored to have this event at the Hotel Arnaud-LeBlanc, just as I feel honored to have had Mimi's dedication to the business and legacy of the hotel for all these years."

Courteous murmurs of agreement circled the room. All attendees, invited or not, seemed pleased with Horace's words. All but one, whose words flew above the soft murmurs like a hawk going in for a kill.

"That's a whole lot of honor from someone who's about to dump the legacy!"

Heads turned from side to side, searching for the source of the brash accusation. Like the others, Sadie and Broussard surveyed the room, curious who had decided to start the verbal food fight they'd hoped would break out. Their eyes found their destination in one inebriated redhead.

"Clotile!" Lisette moved quickly to Clotile's side in an attempt to hush her up. Instead of heeding her friend's warning, Clotile pushed Lisette aside and began walking toward Horace.

"I… I don't know what you're talking about," Horace said. "I love this hotel."

"But you love money more, don't you?"

Sadie and Broussard exchanged looks, eyebrows raised. This was going to be even better than they had thought. Clotile had barely managed a sentence before Johnny Malone jumped in. They'd figured he'd need at least ten minutes of goading before he broke.

"I don't know what you're talking about," Horace said, fighting to keep his composure.

"C'mon, Horace," Clotile said. "Tell everyone what you've been up to. Maybe then they'll understand why we're having this celebration of life to begin with. We should be calling this a celebration of *ending* life, shouldn't we?"

Lisette grabbed Clotile in an attempt to stop the shocking display, but Clotile pushed her away and turned her anger toward Johnny. "And YOU!" she screamed.

"What about me?" Johnny sneered. "Why are you so angry? You missed me too much?"

Horace looked between the two. "You two know each other?"

"You can make that past tense," Clotile said. "Anyone who keeps this guy around is an idiot. You should listen to that if you care about your hotel."

"IF? IF I care about it?" Horace stepped around the table and approached Clotile. "What are you talking about? You don't know me well enough to judge what I love and what I don't."

"Maybe not," Clotile admitted. "But I know the kind of people who go into business with Johnny. They either want to dump their businesses with shady tactics, or they're too stupid to see a scam when it's right in front of their noses."

"You don't know what you're talking about," Horace said. "I wasn't going to sell it. We were forming a new corporation to take care of it. To remodel and restore it."

"Remodel it?" Clotile laughed. "That's what Johnny tells all his clients. Until they sell it short and find out the corporation is a phony and the restored building is turning into private luxury condos."

Confused looks dotted faces of the guests who remained. Many had chosen to depart quickly before things became more volatile. A few grabbed whatever delicacies they could from the buffet on the way out, hunching low as if expecting bullets to fly at any moment.

"Private luxury condos?" Horace was shouting now. "That's impossible. I've seen the blueprints myself. They show just a few minor interior changes."

"Because that's all he's showing you," Clotile said. "Let me ask you this: Did you agree on a final price for the sale yet?"

Horace looked around the room at shocked faces. "We were finalizing that when poor Mimi..." He choked up, unable to speak. Bluette came around the table and put her arm around him, glaring at Clotile for upsetting her uncle.

Broussard held out a plate of appetizers in front of Sadie, who took a miniature crab cake and tossed it into her mouth. Coco's head popped up and settled on the edge of the tote to watch the commotion.

"Why don't you explain, Johnny," Clotile said, turning back to Johnny, who had conveniently edged closer to an emergency exit.

"You'll shut up, Clotile, if you know what's good for you." Johnny took another step toward the exit, but Broussard moved quickly to block the way.

"Like I shut up during the New York deal when the building just happened to burn down right before the price was finalized? Or the Los Angeles deal with the water damage that caused the value to plummet right before the sale closed?"

"You're walking on thin ice, Clotile," Johnny warned.

"No." Clotile stood her ground. "I *was* walking on thin ice then because I didn't know what you were up to. I left Chicago because I found out. I didn't want to be any part of it."

Johnny turned to Broussard. "She's never been very stable, especially after a few drinks."

"Me? Not stable?" Clotile burst into laughter that caused a few to wonder if Johnny had a valid point. "I'm not the one who resorts to drastic measures in order to devalue businesses."

"I told you to shut up, Clotile." Johnny hissed. "You don't want to embarrass Horace in front of all these people, do you?"

"A little late for that," Sadie whispered to the carnation on her lapel.

Horace swiveled abruptly to face Johnny, his face draining of color. A meatball flew off his plate, which Coco tried to catch without success. "*What* drastic measures, Johnny?"

Any murmurs that had been floating around ceased as the room fell silent.

"You tell me, Horace," Johnny said. "You're the one who just happened to return to town when the only remaining member of your rival family happened to die."

Lisette stepped in front of Mimi's photos, as if protecting Mimi from the horrible scene, but kept silent as another voice spoke out.

"How dare you!"

This comment brought the escalating scenario to an abrupt halt. No one had ever heard Bluette raise her voice before. Even Sadie stepped back, stunned.

"My uncle would never hurt anyone, much less Mimi. He loved her!" She turned in a slow circle, making eye contact with everyone in the room as she spoke. "Yes, it's true. My uncle loved Mimi with all his heart. Our stupid families kept them apart. That's why he left. Not because he wasn't devoted to the hotel! He left because his heart was broken."

"I gotta admit I did not see that one coming, Coco," Sadie said, shaking her head.

Lisette now lifted her arm and pointed to Johnny. "Then it was you. You're the one who killed poor Mimi. You slipped into my bakery that morning with the poison. You knew which tart was for her because it had her name on it."

The murmurs around the room started again, mixed with gasps from more than one guest.

"No," Clotile said, drawing eyes to her that had moved from Horace to Johnny.

"Clotile?" Lisette said, eyes growing wide. Horace and Bluette also stared.

"No, I mean it wasn't Johnny," Clotile said.

"Thank you, Clotile," Johnny said, earning a hateful gaze from Clotile.

"Johnny never does his own dirty work," Clotile said. "He always has a sidekick somewhere in the wings."

"Or in this case…" Sadie spoke up as Broussard's two officers dragged a figure in handcuffs into the room "…in the garden."

Again murmurs circled the crowd. Horace, Bluette, Lisette, and Clotile all stared as Sadie walked over to the petite figure dressed in a Cajun Clippers uniform. She calmly removed the person's cap, sunglasses, and dust mask and then turned to face the room.

"Meet Virginia Moretti," Sadie said. "Better known here in New Orleans as Gina, the fortune-teller."

TWENTY-SEVEN

"Great turnout!" Sadie looked around the crowded interior of Chez Lisette Patisserie, pleased to see how many people had shown up to support the bakery reopening. Locals and tourists alike sipped coffee and chicory. Young and elderly feasted on Lisette's mouthwatering beignets, cinnamon rolls, and rice fritters.

Clotile nodded, a partially consumed beignet in one hand and a powdered sugar mustache on her upper lip. "Yes. Lisette is thrilled. And it's so sweet of Bluette to be here this morning to help her out."

Sadie took a sip of her café au lait and sighed. "I feel like such a fool for telling that fortune-teller where I was staying. I've traveled enough to know it's wise to be careful about things like that." A yip of reprimand followed from Coco, whose head and paws hung over the side of the tote bag, nose sniffing the enticing aromas of freshly baked bread and sweets.

"Oh, hush." Sadie teasingly shushed the Yorkie. "She had you under her spell, too, as soon as she read your paw."

"You shouldn't blame yourself," Clotile said. "You had no way of knowing she was fishing for information. In fact, maybe she wasn't. Maybe it only occurred to her at the time that you'd make a convenient decoy."

"She was certainly quite the frail thing, underneath all that gypsy attire," Sadie mused.

"Light enough to zoom out of an alley on a bicycle," Clotile noted.

"And to pull off the gardening disguise," Sadie said. "She sure looked different without that mop of a wig she wore to tell fortunes."

Looking above the cheerful crowd, Sadie noticed Detective Broussard enter and glance around. Spotting Sadie, he crossed the room to join her.

"Good morning, Ms. Kramer," the detective said.

"What, no corsage this time?" Sadie quipped. "And are you ever going to call me Sadie instead of Ms. Kramer?"

"Maybe I'll call you... if I have a question about a case," Broussard said. "How would you feel about that?"

"I suppose that would be okay." Sadie hoped her answer sounded light and casual.

"And what if I don't have a question about a case?" Broussard asked.

Caught off guard, Sadie simply smiled.

"You're blushing," Clotile whispered in Sadie's ear, close enough that Broussard couldn't overhear.

"I think that would be fine," Sadie said to Broussard with just a hint of a smile.

Lisette joined them after delivering an order to a table of women nearby.

"I still can't figure out how you knew the fortune-teller was the killer," Lisette said.

Sadie held up her arm to display the bracelet of skull beads.

"You knew because of a bracelet?"

"Well, I had a slight suspicion because of an incoming phone call Gina received during our second session. It seemed like the same Chicago area code, but I only saw it briefly before she put the phone away," Sadie said. "Then when the police showed me the security tape, I didn't see anything at first. But I asked them to run it again."

"And again… and again," Broussard said.

"Which was when I noticed a light spot around the edge of the person's sleeve," Sadie continued. "It was too faint to tell what it was at first, but I asked the technician to enlarge the image. That's when I recognized this bracelet."

"The one you have on now?" Lisette looked confused.

"Not this exact one!" Sadie laughed. "I'd admired one just like it on Gina's wrist the first time I went to see her. I found *this* one later at a shop down the street. I think it's a good souvenir, don't you?"

"Quite stylish," Clotile said. "In a voodoo sort of way."

"Exactly what I thought," Sadie said. "I may need to order some for Flair, my fashion boutique. The hip clientele would probably go for them."

"Any excuse to shop, right?" Clotile said.

"Of course!" Sadie said. "You should see the mugs I picked up at the French Market. I just had to make a trip back there. Coco even has a new dog bowl. She loved the fleur-de-lis pattern so much that she licked it right in front of the vendor."

"Well, I can see why you bought it." Clotile laughed.

Horace LeBlanc entered, dressed casually compared to the formal attire he wore for Mimi's funeral and reception. He ordered at the counter and then joined other hotel workers at a window table.

Lisette excused herself to go greet Horace and make the rounds to greet others.

"It's nice to see Horace looking more relaxed today," Clotile said. She took another bite of her beignet, this time brushing away the traces of powdered sugar. Coco attempted to catch the sweet falling powder with her tongue.

Broussard agreed. "I'm sure he's relieved to be ruled out as the killer. It did seem suspicious that he reappeared in town at the time of the murder. Not that we didn't have other suspects to investigate." He looked around the ceiling in an amused manner, avoiding eye contact with Clotile.

Clotile laughed and looked at Sadie. "You suspected me too, didn't you?"

"Briefly," Sadie admitted. "It did seem suspicious when you said you were from Chicago since Detective Broussard had pointed out the Chicago area code on the paper Horace dropped."

"I'm sure he's glad to have Mimi's celebration of life event at the hotel over too," Sadie said. "Especially after all that drama."

"Drama that I caused," Clotile admitted. "But I couldn't stand to see Johnny trying to pull off another one of his schemes. He tried to get me involved with those other projects in New York and Los Angeles. I had to quit, even when he tried to bribe me with large amounts of cash to stay and do his dirty work. Burning down one building and destroying another with water damage? Just to devalue the properties so he could pick them up for a bargain? No, thank you."

"Well, Gina isn't as smart or ethical as you are, Clotile," Sadie pointed out. "Really, resorting to murdering a business's key person is crazy."

Broussard nodded. "People can make poor decisions when money is involved. We see it a lot in our line of work." He turned to Clotile. "But it was good that you blew up at Johnny. It helped us solve the case. Those two will be behind bars for a long time."

Turning to Sadie, Broussard continued. "And you got it all on tape, which was extremely helpful. Especially when Gina confessed to sneaking into the bakery *and* your room with the poisoned whipped cream."

"Well, I *did* get to wear that lovely corsage in order to do it." Sadie smiled and then added. "I bet you use that wire-tapping technique all the time, Detective Broussard."

"Actually, it's the first time," Broussard said. "And you're welcome to call me John."

Clotile whispered in Sadie's ear again. "Now *he's* blushing."

"John, as in… Johnny?" Sadie said with a mock frown.

"No." Broussard laughed. "John as in Jean-Pierre. Our family history here goes back many generations."

Lisette returned after working her way around the room, thanking people for coming, and refilling coffee. "Everything turned out just fine." She let out a contented sigh.

"Yes," Sadie agreed. "You have loyal customers and the support of a great community."

"We do stick together here in the Big Easy," Clotile said.

Sadie laughed. "You can all call it the Big Easy if you want. I think I'll be referring to it as the Big Adventure from now on." Coco yipped in agreement.

"Well, it's that too," Clotile admitted.

"It certainly is in my line of work," Broussard said. "A day never goes by without some kind of adventure." He turned to Sadie. "I suspect the same goes for you."

"I will confess that's true," Sadie said.

Lisette held up one finger, indicating she'd be right back. She retreated behind the counter, set a few items on a tray, and returned.

"Beignets and café au lait for all of us," she said, presenting four steaming cups and a plate of the legendary treats.

Each person took a cup and a beignet. Lisette did the same, setting the tray down and facing the others. Holding up her café au lait, she proclaimed, "To adventure."

All four cups clicked as Sadie, Broussard, Clotile, and Lisette toasted together.

"To adventure!"

A Flair For Beignets

Lisette's Beignets

Ingredients:

1 cup water
1 cup milk
1 egg
1 teaspoon vanilla
3 cups all-purpose flour
2 tablespoons baking powder
1 teaspoon salt
3 teaspoons sugar
Large pinch nutmeg
4 cups oil for frying
Powdered sugar to dust

Directions:

Mix water, milk, egg, and vanilla.

Sift together dry ingredients and add to wet mixture, mixing well until batter is smooth.

Drop by spoonfuls into hot oil and gently turn until brown and puffy.

Drain beignets on a paper towel and dust with powdered sugar.

Enjoy with your café au lait!

Acknowledgements

Sadie Kramer and Coco have a great time on their fictional adventures, but they only manage to do so with the help of very real people.

I owe heartfelt thanks to Annie Sarac at The Editing Pen for polishing up the rough edges of *A Flair for Beignets*. Keri Knutson of Alchemy Book Covers and Design deserves a round of applause for the lively, colorful covers that grace all the Sadie Kramer Flair Mysteries. Formatting credit goes to Tara Meyers. Beta readers Jay Garner, Louise Martens, Tara Meyers, and Carol Anderson all provided insight into story development. And Paul Sterrett deserves a medal of patience for enduring my daily chatter about the plot for months on end.

If you're looking to enjoy some delicious beignets just like Sadie and her New Orleans friends do in this story, put on your patisserie hat and have some fun. The beignet recipe provided is courtesy of Keri Knutson, who not only works magic with graphic design but also knows her way around the kitchen.

As always, I'm grateful for the support of amazing family, friends, and readers in my life. Their encouragement is what allows Sadie and Coco to enjoy a world of mystery.

Books by Deborah Garner

The Paige MacKenzie Series

Above the Bridge

When NY reporter Paige MacKenzie arrives in Jackson Hole, it's not long before her instincts tell her there's more than a basic story to be found in the popular, northwestern Wyoming mountain area. A chance encounter with attractive cowboy Jake Norris soon has Paige chasing a legend of buried treasure passed down through generations. Side- stepping a few shady characters who are also searching for the same hidden reward, she will have to decide who is trustworthy and who is not.

The Moonglow Café

The discovery of an old diary inside the wall of the historic hotel soon sends NY reporter Paige MacKenzie into the underworld of art and deception. Each of the town's residents holds a key to untangling more than one long-buried secret, from the hippie chick owner of a new age café to the mute homeless man in the town park. As the worlds of western art and sapphire mining collide, Paige finds herself juggling research, romance, and danger.

Three Silver Doves

The New Mexico resort of Agua Encantada seems a perfect destination for reporter Paige MacKenzie to combine work with well-deserved rest and relaxation. But when suspicious jewelry shows up on another guest, and the town's storyteller goes missing, Paige's R&R is soon redefined as restlessness and risk. Will an unexpected overnight trip to Tierra Roja Casino lead her to the answers she seeks, or are darker secrets lurking along the way?

Hutchins Creek Cache

When a mysterious 1920's coin is discovered behind the Hutchins Creek Railroad Museum in Colorado, Paige MacKenzie starts digging into four generations of Hutchins family history, with a little help from the Denver Mint. As legends of steam engines and coin mintage mingle, will Paige discover the true origin of the coin, or will she find herself riding the rails dangerously close to more than one long-hidden town secret?

Crazy Fox Ranch

As Paige MacKenzie returns to Jackson Hole, she has only two things on her mind: enjoy life with Wyoming's breathtaking Grand Tetons as the backdrop, and spend more time with handsome cowboy Jake Norris as he prepares to open his guest ranch. But when a stranger's odd behavior leads her to research western filming in the area—in particular, the movie *Shane*, will it simply lead to a freelance article for the *Manhattan Post*, or will it lead to a dangerous hidden secret?

The Sadie Kramer Flair Series

A Flair for Chardonnay

When flamboyant senior sleuth Sadie Kramer learns the owner of her favorite chocolate shop is in trouble, she heads for the California wine country with a tote-bagged Yorkie and a slew of questions. The fourth-generation Tremiato Winery promises answers, but not before a dead body turns up at the vintners' scheduled Harvest Festival. As Sadie juggles truffles, tips, and turmoil, she'll need to sort the grapes from the wrath in order to find the identity of the killer.

A Flair for Drama

When a former schoolmate invites Sadie Kramer to a theatre production, she jumps at the excuse to visit the Monterey Bay area for a weekend. Plenty of action is expected on stage, but when the show's leading lady turns up dead, Sadie finds herself faced with more than one drama to follow. With both cast members and production crew as potential suspects, will Sadie and her sidekick Yorkie, Coco, be able to solve the case?

A Flair for Beignets

With fabulous music, exquisite cuisine, and rich culture, how could a week in New Orleans be anything less than fantastic for Sadie Kramer and her sidekick Yorkie, Coco? And it is... until a customer at a popular patisserie drops dead face-first in a raspberry-almond tart. A competitive bakery, a newly formed friendship, and even her hotel's luxurious accommodations offer possible suspects. As Sadie sorts through a gumbo of interconnected characters, will she discover who the killer is, or will the killer discover her first?

A Flair for Truffles

Sadie Kramer's friendly offer to deliver three boxes of gourmet Valentines truffles for her neighbor's chocolate shop backfires when she arrives to find the intended recipient deceased. Even more intriguing is the fact that the elegant heart-shaped gifts were ordered by three different men. With the help of one detective and the hindrance of another, Sadie will search San Francisco for clues. But will she find out "whodunit" before the killer finds a way to stop her?

A Flair for Flip-Flops

When the body of a heartthrob celebrity washes up on the beach outside Sadie Kramer's luxury hotel suite, her fun in the sun soon turns into sleuthing with the stars. The resort's wine and appetizer gatherings, suspicious guest behavior, and casual strolls along the beach boardwalk may provide clues, but will they be enough to discover who the killer is, or will mystery and mayhem leave a Hollywood scandal unsolved?

The Moonglow Christmas Series

Mistletoe at Moonglow

The small town of Timberton, Montana, hasn't been the same since resident chef and artist, Mist, arrived, bringing a unique new age flavor to the old western town. When guests check in for the holidays, they bring along worries, fears, and broken hearts, unaware that Mist has a way of working magic in people's lives. One thing is certain: no matter how cold winter's grip is on each guest, no one leaves Timberton without a warmer heart.

Silver Bells at Moonglow

Christmas brings an eclectic gathering of visitors and locals to the Timberton Hotel each year, guaranteeing an eventful season. Add in a hint of romance, and there's more than snow in the air around the small Montana town. When the last note of Christmas carols has faded away, the soft whisper of silver bells from the front door's wreath will usher guests and townsfolk back into the world with hope for the coming year.

Gingerbread at Moonglow

The Timberton Hotel boasts an ambiance of near-magical proportions during the Christmas season. As the aromas of ginger, cinnamon, nutmeg, and molasses mix with heartfelt camaraderie and sweet romance, holiday guests share reflections on family, friendship, and life. Will decorating the outside of a gingerbread house prove easier than deciding what goes inside?

Nutcracker Sweets at Moonglow

When a nearby theatre burns down just before Christmas, cast members of *The Nutcracker* arrive at the Timberton Hotel with only a sliver of holiday joy. Camaraderie, compassion, and shared inspiration combine to help at least one hidden dream come true. As with every Christmas season, this year's guests will face the New Year with a renewed sense of hope.

Snowfall at Moonglow

As holiday guests arrive at the Timberton Hotel with hopes of a white Christmas, unseasonably warm weather hints at a less-than-wintery wonderland. But whether the snow falls or not, one thing is certain: with resident artist and chef, Mist, around, there's bound to be a little magic. No one ever leaves Timberton without renewed hope for the future.

Stand-alone: *Cranberry Bluff*

Molly Elliott's quiet life is disrupted when routine errands land her in the middle of a bank robbery. Accused and cleared of the crime, she flees both media attention and mysterious, threatening notes to run a bed and breakfast on the Northern California coast. Her new beginning is peaceful until five guests show up at the inn, each with a hidden agenda. As true motives become apparent, will Molly's past come back to haunt her, or will she finally be able to leave it behind?

For more information on Deborah Garner's books:
Facebook: https://www.facebook.com/deborahgarnerauthor
Twitter: https://twitter.com/PaigeandJake
Website: http://deborahgarner.com
Mailing list: http://bit.ly/deborahgarner